I0546038

The story, all names, characters, and incidents portrayed in this production are fictitious. No identification with actual persons (living or deceased) is intended or should be inferred.

First paperback edition: June 2025

Book cover by Flux-1

ISBN   978-1-9680275-1-3 (6x9 paperback)
ISBN   978-1-9680275-2-0 (6x9 hardback)

The

Survivor's

Apocalypse

Part II
The Sisterhood of Wives

M.P. Hendy

Table of Contents

Chapter 13: The morning after...3

Chapter 14: Caught red handed 22

Chapter 15: The pig pen project 40

Chapter 16: The Callie fornication girl...................................58

Chapter 17: Grace's Strategic Siege 77

Chapter 18: The foundations of David....................................95

Chapter 19: The forge and the well......................................113

Chapter 20: The gunsmith's fiancé.......................................132

Chapter 21: The project of affection.....................................151

Chapter 22: The Beast's wild harvest....................................171

Chapter 23: The weakest daughter 191

Chapter 24: The sniper's bullet 209

Appendix: 2..227

Chapter 13:

The Morning After

Kyle jolted awake, half laying on his couch. The rhythmic thwack thwack of the Mortal Kombat theme from the main menu filled the otherwise quiet apartment. He blinked, trying to dispel the lingering haze of the wine and whatever…dream?…he'd been having.

He looked at his surroundings. Grace was still sitting next to him, her legs draped across his lap, her head lolling gently against the arm of the couch. She looked peaceful, like a sleeping angel, an angel wearing his oversized gray t-shirt. Kyle swallowed, trying to ignore the warmth that was spreading through him. His hands were instinctively tucked between her thighs, her smaller hand holding his, a comfortable, innocent hold. He hadn't even realized he'd fallen asleep like this. He glanced at the clock on the wall, nearly 9:30. Time had slipped away. An hour had vanished since dinner, since the last of the wine, since the playful banter and the way Grace's laughter had echoed in the small apartment, making it feel less like a bunker and more like a home.

He felt a deep sense of contentment, a quiet joy that had been building throughout the evening. They'd talked about everything and nothing, from the mundane ranch operations to the impossible future, to their shared love for old video games. Grace, with her sweet disposition and observant eyes, had a way of making him feel completely at ease, completely himself. She loved him like a wife, a casual domesticity that Kyle found himself increasingly drawn to. It was easy, comfortable, and profoundly good.

Kyle swallowed, the comfortable contentment momentarily replaced by a jolt of...something else. He glanced down at Grace, still sound asleep. The dim light from the flickering screen cast long shadows, but even in the muted glow, he could see that her shirt had ridden up, exposing a sliver of smooth, bare skin just above her waist. It was innocent, unintentional, and yet...it was undeniably alluring. He carefully shifted his weight, intending to gently tug the shirt back down. He didn't want to wake her, and he certainly didn't want to be caught staring.

As he moved his hand, Grace stirred slightly. Her grip on his tightened, a small, almost imperceptible squeeze. Her eyes remained closed, her breathing still deep and even, but the pressure on his hand was undeniable. She wasn't fully asleep. "Mmm," she murmured, her voice thick with sleep. "Don't move." Kyle froze, his heart skipping a beat. "Grace?" he whispered, unsure if she was truly awake or just in some liminal space between dreams.

There was a pause, a beat of silence punctuated only by the sporadic sound effects from the paused video game. Then, her voice, softer and more vulnerable than he'd ever heard it, drifted up to him. "Do you...do you want to go to bed?" The question hung in the air, heavy with unspoken meaning. Kyle's mind raced. Bed. It wasn't just about sleep, not with Grace. It was about intimacy, about crossing a threshold they'd been dancing around for years. It was about acknowledging the undeniable physical pull that had been simmering beneath the surface of their comfortable companionship.

Kyle's breath hitched in his throat as Grace's grip on his hand tightened, pulling him forward. Before he could fully process her whispered question, she made the decision for him. With an effortless grace that belied her slender frame, she shifted, her arm coiling around his neck, and then, with a surprising but gentle surge of power, she pulled.

He tumbled forward, a soft landing, squarely on her. The impact was cushioned by her body, a paradox of yielding softness and undeniable strength. He felt the firm curve of her hip against his, the warmth of her bare leg as it wrapped around him, drawing him even closer, until his chest was pressed against her. The faint scent of her shampoo, a mix of wildflowers and sun, filled his nostrils, intoxicating him further than the wine already had.

Her eyes, which had been closed, now fluttered open, bright and luminous in the dim light. There was a directness in their gaze, an unyielding certainty that stole whatever remaining breath Kyle had. The mild drunkenness that had been a pleasant haze now intensified, not in a woozy way, but in a rush of heat and a dizzying sense of freefall. Then, slowly, intimately, and with an intention that left no room for misinterpretation, Grace's lips met his. It wasn't a tentative brush, or a playful peck. It was a deliberate claim, soft at first, a gentle pressure that spoke of tenderness, but with an underlying current of fierce desire.

Then, with an unhurried, almost languid grace, her tongue slipped into his mouth. It was a revelation, a soft, probing invasion that stole his free will, dissolving the last vestiges of his self-control. A shiver, both of shock and profound pleasure, coursed through him. The mild buzz now felt like a roaring inferno in his veins, setting every nerve ending alight. He felt his own lips part in invitation, his body instinctively arching closer, seeking more of the intoxicating connection.

Kyle was acutely aware that Grace's softness and tenderness was entirely intentional. She was quick, agile, and stronger than most strong men, a fact he'd witnessed firsthand during training and even during missions. The way she'd pulled him onto her, so effortlessly, spoke volumes. Her gentleness now, the way her hand cradled the back of his head, her fingers tangling in his hair with a surprising delicacy, was a conscious choice. She was showing him her soft side, inviting him, not overwhelming him, despite her immense physical capability. It was a profound act of trust, a testament to her desire to be cherished, even as she was the one taking control.

Grace paused for a moment, breaking the kiss. She looked into Kyle's eyes, her expression a mixture of affection and vulnerability. "You alright?" she asked, gently stroking his hair. Kyle swallowed hard, his throat suddenly dry. He ran a hand through his own hair, feeling the lingering warmth of her touch. "Yeah, I'm...more than alright." He managed a shaky smile. It was the understatement of the century. He found it difficult to even look away from her because her eyes were so beautiful.

Grace chuckled softly, a melodic sound that vibrated through him. "Good. Because I want this, Kyle. All of it." She shifted slightly. "Do you want me?" He closed his eyes for a split second, gathering his thoughts. The question, so simple, so direct, hit him with the force of a tidal wave. "Grace," he began, his voice a little raspy. "You know I want you. But…" Grace gently placed her fingers over his lips, silencing him. "Don't. Don't you dare bring up the age thing, or anything else that doesn't matter. Not right now. Not ever. I know what I want, Kyle. And what I want…is you."

He covered her hand with his, his thumb tracing the delicate bones of her wrist. And he kissed her again. After a moment, Grace pulled back slightly, a playful sparkle in her eyes as she began to caress his neck. "You know, I've wanted to be your woman for a long time, Kyle. Even back when you were crushing on Taylor." Kyle's eyes widened in surprise. "You…you knew about that?" He felt a flush creep up his neck. It felt silly and a bit embarrassing to be reminded of a crush from so long ago.

Grace nodded, a knowing smile playing on her lips. "Of course, I knew. I see everything, Kyle. You made it pretty obvious." She leaned in closer, her voice a low whisper. "But even then," she continued, "even with you and your brother mooning over Taylor and Jennifer, I knew there was something special about you. Something kind, something strong, something…mine." Grace's words, delivered in that whisper, wrapped around Kyle like a warm embrace, tightening with each word. Something kind, something strong, something...mine. The possessiveness in her voice wasn't off-putting; it was a soft, undeniable claim, a declaration that stirred something ancient and protective within him.

He swallowed hard, his mind a jumble of emotions. Shock, tenderness, a potent surge of desire that warred with the ingrained sense of understanding. Yet, looking into her eyes, those intelligent, knowing eyes that had seen through his youthful infatuation with Taylor, he found it impossible to argue. She did see everything. "Grace," he breathed, a tremor running through him. She didn't let him speak, her gaze never leaving his. Her fingers, slid up to cup his cheek, her thumb caressing the stubble there. "I love you, Kyle," she stated, her voice clear now, unwavering, each word a soft, heavy stone dropped into the quiet space between them. It wasn't a question, or a plea, but a simple, profound statement of fact. "I have for a long time. Longer than you know, maybe even longer than I fully understood myself. But I know it, truly. Every part of me loves every part of you."

His breath hitched. He had, in his own way, loved her for a while too. A protective, fond love that had grown subtly, insidiously, into something much deeper. He'd seen her grow from a quiet, observant girl into this self-assured, beautiful woman, and he'd admired her, cared for her, felt an inexplicable pull towards her. But to hear her say it, so openly, so completely... it was overwhelming.

Grace's lips found his, soft and yielding, yet with an underlying current of intense purpose. Her tongue, nimble and confident, traced the seam of his lips, a silent invitation he couldn't refuse. His own lips parted, and her tongue entered, a warm, soft invasion. Her hand, previously cupping his cheek, slid gracefully behind his neck, her fingers tangling in the short hairs there, pulling him closer, deepening the kiss further still. He responded instinctively, his own hand finding her waist, pulling her flush against him.

As the kiss intensified, a curious sensation registered against his palm. His hand, still firmly on her waist, had begun to slide, following the curve of her hip. The soft, worn cotton of his gray t-shirt, which she wore, seemed to be bunching, riding up. He registered the sensation vaguely, his mind too flooded with the kiss to truly focus. But then, as her hips shifted slightly, his fingers brushed against smooth, warm skin. Not cotton. Skin.

His eyes, which had been closed, fluttered open. The kiss was still rich and consuming, but a part of his brain, the part that handled basic sensory input, was screaming. He pulled back fractionally, just enough to break the direct contact of their lips, though their foreheads still rested together, their breaths mingling. His gaze dropped, drawn by an irresistible curiosity.

And there it was. His gray t-shirt, the one Grace had put on after her shower, was indeed pushed up, bunched around her mid-chest. Below it, her stomach was flat, her navel a small, dark swirl. Her hips, just under his hand, were bare, smooth, and exquisitely curved. She was completely naked from the chest down, the shirt more of a suggestion than an actual covering. The soft glow of the lights cast a warm sheen on her skin.

Grace noticed his sudden stillness, the widening of his eyes. A soft giggle escaped her lips. "Like what you see?" she asked, her voice a seductive whisper. A playful smile danced on her face, as she said, "Look at me, Kyle." Kyle felt a blush creep up his neck. He knew what she wanted. He knew what everyone expected. He started to turn away, shame burning in his chest. "Grace, I…" he began, but she stopped him, her hand gently cupping his cheek. "Kyle," she said softly, her thumb tracing the line of his jaw. Her gaze was unwavering, confident. "Don't."

Before he could voice his turmoil, Grace spoke again, her voice laced with a sultry confidence that belied her age. "Look at me, Kyle," she repeated, her hand moving to gently tug the t-shirt even higher, revealing more of her smooth skin. "Look at it. After all," she murmured, her breath warm against his ear, "this all belongs to you."

And then, she did it. Grace pulled Kyle's face down, guiding him with a strength that surprised him, a gentle force he couldn't resist. Her naked breasts pressed against his mouth, soft and yielding. He gasped, his mind reeling. The scent of her skin, the warmth against his lips, it was overwhelming. He closed his eyes, trying to reconcile the innocence he remembered with the woman she was becoming.

He opened his eyes, looking up at Grace. Her eyes were half-closed, a soft moan escaping her lips. The moment was intoxicating, terrifying. He wanted to yield, to succumb to the overwhelming desire that threatened to consume him. But something held him back. Grace, sensing Kyle's hesitation again, slid out from under him. She paused, her gaze unwavering, searching his face for a moment. Then, without a word, she bent down, wrapped her arms around him, and lifted him off his feet.

Kyle yelped in surprise, his arms instinctively wrapping around her neck. He was completely weightless in her arms, like a child being carried by a parent. The strength she possessed was surreal, a constant reminder of their unusual family. Grace carried Kyle to his bed like a toddler and dropped him gently onto the mattress. He bounced slightly, staring up at her, a mixture of awe and fear in his eyes. Her terrifying strength nearly paralyzed him.

He sat up, speechless. "Grace," he finally managed to stammer, "What...what was that?" Grace stood over him, her expression a mixture of amusement, frustration, and a possessiveness that made his heart skip a beat. "Just a reminder, Kyle," she said softly, her voice laced with a hint of steel. "That I'm stronger. That I want you. That you're mine."

She took a step closer, her eyes boring into his, the frustration now clearer, more potent than the amusement. "And a reminder," she continued, her voice gaining a sharper edge, "that the only roadblock holding us back, the only hurdle, is the one you keep hiding behind. It's not real, Kyle. Not to me. Not to David. Not to anyone who matters here. It's just your fear, your hang-up." Her words hung in the air, a direct challenge to his internal struggle, a clear expression of her exasperation with his hesitation. She wasn't asking anymore; she was stating a fact, laying bare his own self-imposed barrier.

Before he could find the words, Grace moved. Her hands, surprisingly gentle despite her overwhelming strength, reached for the drawstring of his pajama pants. His breath hitched. He knew what was coming, and a jolt of pure, unadulterated panic shot through him. At the same time, a tidal wave of anticipation washed over him, threatening to drown every last vestige of resistance. With a swift, practiced movement, she untied the knot and slid the pajama pants down his legs, leaving him exposed. He lay there, naked and trembling, his eyes locked on hers.

The soft glow of the faint light cast long, dancing shadows across Kyle's room as Grace, with a single, fluid motion, pulled the grey t-shirt over her head. The fabric peeled away from her skin, revealing the toned expanse of her back, the curve of her waist, and the subtle flex of muscles that hinted at the astonishing power hidden beneath. Kyle's eyes widened, following the descent of the shirt until it landed in a silent heap on the floor, leaving her standing before him in nothing but the ethereal luminescence of the room. Every line of her body was a testament to natural beauty and an almost mythological strength.

Then, with an agility that made him jump, she was moving before he could even register it. A whisper of air, a shift in the ambient light, and she was no longer standing but kneeling, straddling him on the bed. The mattress dipped slightly under her weight, but her balance was impeccable, her posture regal even as she leaned forward, her face inches from his. Her gaze, intense and unwavering, held his captive. There was no shyness in her eyes, no trace of the young girl. And in this moment, she saw his fear, his desire, and the last remnants of his resistance.

Her hands moved again. Behind her back, the crinkle of foil the loudest sound in the suddenly hushed room. His breath hitched, a gasp trapped in his throat as she brought her hand down, her cool, soft touch a shiver against his skin. He felt the light pressure as she sheathed him, her touch firm and confident, utterly devoid of hesitation. There was a brief, almost imperceptible adjustment, a final, intimate touch that sent a jolt through his entire body. His cock, already standing at attention, throbbed with a mixture of nervous apprehension and burgeoning desire.

Grace leaned closer, her eyes, usually so sweet and observant, now held a predatory gleam, like a cat ready to pounce on its prey. "Kyle," she whispered, her voice a deep rumble that seemed to vibrate directly through him, bypassing his ears and going straight to his soul. It was a voice he hadn't heard from her before. "Do you know why I'm here?" He swallowed, his throat dry. "Grace…" he started, but the name caught, a choked sound.

A soft smile touched her lips, a knowing curve that softened the intensity of her gaze just enough to be tender. "Because after tonight," she continued, "there is nothing separating us." Her hands, which had been resting lightly on his thighs, tightened, her fingers digging in just enough to send a ripple of sensation through his skin. Not forceful, but utterly purposeful. Her eyes bored into his, holding him captive. "Not society, Kyle. Not the whispers or the sideways glances. Not my father, and certainly not your sister." And then she delivered the final blow, the one that shattered the last remnants of his resistance, her voice dropping to a fierce, almost guttural growl. "And not my fucking age."

Then, with a slow, deliberate grace, she began to lower herself. He felt the first brush of her slick heat against the tip of him, a searing sensation that stole his breath. A gasp tore from his throat as she slid down, inch by excruciating inch, her body warm and wet, enclosing him in a sheath of pure sensation. The world narrowed to the feel of her, the perfect fit, the exquisite pressure. He was filling her, and she was taking him, utterly, completely, without hesitation. It was a sensation unlike anything he had ever known, a profound intimacy that resonated deep within his bones.

Grace, now completely filled, leaned close to Kyle's face, her eyes locked onto his, a possessive fire burning in their depths. Her breath, warm against his lips, was uneven, a testament to the powerful moment they were sharing. "Now, fuck your wife, Kyle," she said, her voice a low, gravelly command that resonated through him, vibrating through his very bones. It wasn't a request; it was a declaration, a powerful assertion of their new reality, a breaking of the final chain.

The early morning sun streamed through the single French door window in the expansive room, pooling on the worn carpet. Bonnie stirred, a groan catching in her throat as she stretched, her limbs protesting. Her eyes fluttered open, blinking against the unfamiliar light. She was in a bed, a very comfortable one, but not her bed. And the t-shirt she was wearing… it was huge. Like, several sizes. Definitely not hers.

A glance to her side confirmed the obvious: Seth. He was sprawled on his back, a peaceful expression on his boyish face, soft pajamas rumpled around him. The realization hit her in a warm, embarrassed wave. They had fallen asleep here. After the caverns. After the kiss. And the making out in Aidan's car. Oh, God, Aidan's car.

Bonnie's cheeks flushed a furious red. She hadn't exactly gotten home last night. Her dad, Eric, was either going to be furious or overly concerned. Probably both. She gently nudged Seth's shoulder. "Seth," she whispered, her voice a little croaky. "Seth, wake up." He mumbled something indistinguishable, burying his face deeper into the pillow. Bonnie tried again, a bit firmer this time. "Seth! It's morning.

Seth finally blinked awake, his bright eyes, usually so observant, slowly focusing on her. A sleepy smile tugged at his lips. "Morning, Bonnie." He stretched, a contented sigh escaping him. "You look comfy." "Comfy and… tiny," Bonnie said, gesturing vaguely at the oversized garment. "Is this yours?" Seth chuckled, pushing himself up on an elbow. "Relax. It's mine. You looked tired last night. You fell asleep pretty fast after we got back." His gaze dropped to her face, a hint of the previous night's boldness in his eyes. "Did you sleep well?"

Bonnie felt her stomach do a little flip. "Yeah, I… I did." She looked around the huge room, taking in the second, untouched bed on the far side. "This room is massive. Why two beds?" Seth, still smiling, just nodded towards the other side of the room. "Siblings." Bonnie's brows furrowed. Siblings? She knew David had a lot of kids, but she couldn't immediately place a boy who would share a room with Seth. Lucas was still a baby, wasn't he? "Lucas?" she ventured, already feeling silly for asking. Seth chuckled, a warm, sleepy sound. "Nah, that's Grace's bed. The babies have the other room."

Bonnie blinked. Grace? Seth's twin sister. "Grace?" she repeated, a little incredulously. "You… you share a room with Grace? With a teenage girl?" Seth just shrugged, a hint of amusement in his eyes. "We're twins, Bonnie. We've always shared. Besides," he leaned in conspiratorially, "considering last night was date night, I'd bet money she's probably with Kyle anyway." He said, and Bonnie's face went even hotter.

He sat up fully now, stretching his arms above his head, muscles flexing under the thin fabric of his t-shirt. "And it's not like we have cooties or gross habits," he added, a playful smirk spreading across his face. She suddenly felt a familiar knot tighten in her stomach, pushing past the giddy warmth from their kiss in the caverns. It wasn't just the sheer awkwardness of the sleeping arrangements. It was the looming shadow of her dad, Eric. "My dad," she mumbled, the words practically swallowed by her anxiety. "He's… he's going to kill me."

Seth, still comfortably stretched on his bed, watched her with those observant, kind eyes. He picked up his phone and tossed it lightly, and Bonnie instinctively caught it. "Check," Seth said simply, a knowing smirk playing on his lips. He nodded towards the screen. "I figured you'd be worried."

Bonnie stared at the phone in her hand, then back at Seth's calm, unconcerned face. A flicker of hope, tiny but insistent, sparked within her. She fumbled with the screen, finding the messaging app already open to a conversation with 'Eric'. Her breath hitched. Seth: "Bonnie made it home safe, we had fun. She fell asleep, I'll let her sleep in Grace's room." Bonnie's eyes widened. He had told him? Her heart pounded. This was it. This was where the lecture began, right there in text. She braced herself, scrolling down to see Eric's response. Eric: "Thank you, son, I can't thank you enough. I also had a date last night, so I guess we're looking out for each other."

Bonnie froze. Her eyes scanned the message again. And again. "Thank you son." Her dad called Seth… son? And then the second part hit her like a playful smack in the face. "I also had a date last night, so I guess we're looking out for each other." She slowly lifted her gaze from the phone to Seth, her expression a bewildered mix of shock, relief, and utter, utter confusion. The anxiety that had been coiling in her gut unraveled, replaced by a bubbling, incredulous laughter. "Who? Who would my dad go on a date with?!" Seth shrugged, a picture of nonchalance. "Well, he didn't say who. But I have a pretty good guess."

Bonnie leaned in, utterly captivated. "Who? Tell me!" "Think about it," Seth began, shifting slightly, looking directly at her. "Who does he spend time with? Who's around his age? Who's a single parent, just like him?" Bonnie's eyebrows shot up. "Lynn?!" she practically shrieked, then clapped a hand over her mouth, glancing towards the door as if Grace might suddenly appear, roused by the outburst.

Seth nodded. Bonnie slumped back against the pillow, the phone still clutched in her hand. "My dad... and Lynn." The idea, at first preposterous, began to settle. "Huh. I mean, she's okay. And Josh is cool. But... really? A date?" "Why not?" Seth countered, his voice softer now, more thoughtful. "He deserves someone. Maybe it's not... David-level romance or anything," he chuckled, "but it's companionship. And that's pretty important out here, isn't it?"

Bonnie considered this, her laughter subsiding into a comfortable silence. Seth was right. In the chaotic world they now lived in, companionship was a precious commodity. And her dad, who'd been a single dad for so long, deserved some happiness. The unexpected double-date revelation from her father was oddly... comforting. It took the spotlight off her little adventure.

A slow smile spread across her face. "So, you're saying... while I was out breaking curfew with you," she nudged him playfully with her foot, "my dad was out on a date with Lynn?" Seth chuckled. "That's what it sounds like, doesn't it?" He picked at a loose thread on his blanket. "Though, I bet ours was way more exciting." "Oh, definitely," Bonnie agreed, a smug grin spreading across her face. "The caverns were cool, but Aidan's car was way better for... well, you know."

"I bet they just had a really boring dinner. Like, discussing the merits of different types of fence posts or

18

something equally thrilling." Bonnie snorted, a laugh bubbling up. "Oh my god, you're probably right! My dad would totally do that. 'So, Lynn, how about those solar panels? Really harnessing the sun, aren't we?'" She mimicked her father's earnest tone, then dissolved into giggles.

She scooted closer, a confident grace in her movements, and settled onto Seth's lap, facing him. Her hands tangling in the short hairs at his nape. "You know," Bonnie whispered, her voice a soft murmur against his lips, "I think our romance is already way more eventful than theirs will ever be."

Seth chuckled, a nervous energy bubbling beneath his amusement. Her words were barely out before her lips found his again, a soft, exploring pressure that quickly deepened. It was a kiss far too mature for a couple of teenagers, more akin to something from one of the erotic romance novels Jessica kept in her library. Bonnie shifted, pressing closer, her small body radiating warmth and a surprising intensity. Seth, caught in the moment, wrapped his arms around her waist, pulling her tighter, completely lost in the sweet, thrilling sensation.

It was precisely at this idyllic, utterly scandalous moment that the bedroom door swung open. Not with a dramatic creak, but with the quiet, practiced motion of someone assuming everyone was still asleep. A soft gasp, barely audible, broke through the haze of adolescent desire. Seth's eyes, still half-closed, fluttered open. Bonnie, startled by the sudden stillness in him, pulled back slightly, her own eyes wide and unfocused. They both looked towards the door, their faces flushed, hair slightly mussed, and lips glistening.

Standing in the doorway, a laundry basket hooked over one arm, was Nicole. Her sweet, trusting face, was a tableau of utter bewilderment. Her mouth slightly open, and the laundry basket, filled with neatly folded towels, seemed to list precariously. "Seth? Bonnie?" she managed, her voice a reedy whisper. Her gaze sharpened slightly, though her tone remained gentle, laced with a new kind of directness. "Children," she began, the word a soft reprimand, "I... I think I just walked into something. So... did you two have sex?"

The question hung in the air, a blunt, unavoidable truth. Seth's eyes nearly bugged out of his head. Bonnie let out a high-pitched squeak, shaking her head so vigorously her hair slapped Seth in the face. "Mom! No! Of course not!" Seth blurted, scrambling backward on the bed as if proximity to Bonnie would somehow confirm the accusation. "We were just... talking! And, uh, Bonnie got something in her eye!" He gestured vaguely towards Bonnie's still-pouting lips.

Bonnie, recovering slightly, nodded vigorously. "Yes! A... a dust bunny! Right in my eye!" She blinked rapidly, as if attempting to dislodge an invisible speck. Nicole's lips twitched slightly, a ghost of a smile she quickly suppressed. Oh, bless their innocent, terrible lies. She'd heard better from Poppy trying to explain why she had chocolate smeared all over her face. "A dust bunny that required... vigorous mouth-to-mouth resuscitation, it seems," she murmured, her eyes twinkling betrayingly.

She sighed, then, a soft, warm sigh that wasn't annoyed, but simply... tired. Tired in the way only a parent dealing with the twins could be. Her gaze swept around the room again, taking in the rumpled sheets, clothes on the floor, the general air of clandestine activity. And then, her eyes landed on the other bed in the room, Grace's.

It was meticulously made, as always, but something was off. The pillow looked... untouched. The blanket was folded with a precision that suggested it hadn't been slept under. Grace, the early riser, wasn't there. Nicole's brow furrowed. Grace was usually up by now. A knot of concern tightened in Nicole's stomach, quickly overshadowing the comedic interlude she'd just walked into.

"And where's your sister, Seth?" Nicole asked, her voice losing its playful edge, replaced by a more serious tone. Her eyes, no longer fixed on her son's red face, now scanned the empty space where Grace should have been.

Chapter 14:

Caught Red Handed

The first thing Grace registered was not the gentle morning light filtering through the window, nor the distant chirping of birds simulated by the bunker's impeccable environment controls. No, the very first thing was the distinct, masculine scent of Kyle's bedding, mingled with something undeniably... hers. And the soreness. Oh, the glorious, profound soreness that permeated every muscle from her neck down to her toes. Her eyelids fluttered open, then squeezed shut again as the memories of the previous night came flooding back in a delightful, dizzying rush. Mortal Kombat, romantic dinner, whispered confessions, and then... a blur of skin, sighs, and something akin to fireworks exploding behind her eyes. Non-stop intimacy, indeed.

It was morning. And she was still in Kyle's bed, in Kyle's apartment, a full five minute walk away from her own, which, she suddenly remembered with a horrifying clarity, had an untouched bed. Her eyes snapped open. Kyle was sprawled beside her, a contented, sleepy smile on his face, one arm flung out as if still reaching for her. He looked utterly peaceful, annoyingly so. She, on the other hand, felt a frantic energy buzz beneath her skin. Nicole! Her mom was an early riser, observant, and with a supernatural ability to sniff out anything amiss. Grace's mind raced. What time was it? Had anyone noticed she was gone? The dread coiled tighter in her stomach than a freshly spooled fishing line.

With a silent, practiced grace, Grace slid out of bed, wincing slightly as her feet touched the cool carpet. Every movement was a strategic maneuver against the ache. She glanced back at Kyle, who remained blissfully asleep, a rumpled hero in a sea of tangled sheets. Bless his heart, he was dead to the world. That meant the clean-up operation was entirely her responsibility. The room was, predictably, a disaster zone. Clothes were strewn like discarded battle flags condom wrappers, Kyle's shirt, items she couldn't quite identify from the night's energetic disrobing. The faint scent of their shared passion still clung to the air, a tell-tale sign that screamed "evidence!" Grace moved like a ninja on a mission, scooping up her scattered clothes first, stuffing them into an armful. Then, she tackled Kyle's, tossing them into his hamper.

She took her dress from the chair by the door and put it back on, her fingers fumbling with the buttons. As she did, her eyes darted to the small clock on Kyle's nightstand. 7:15 AM. A gasp caught in her throat. Her mom, Nicole, was usually up and about, making rounds, by 6:30 at the absolute latest. She checked the clock again, a frantic whisper of "No, no, no," escaping her lips. It was too late. She was already busted. The untouched bed, the missing Grace, her mom's radar… it was all over. The five-minute walk felt like a light-year under these circumstances.

A wave of surprisingly calm resignation washed over her. What was the point in trying to sneak back in now? The damage was done. The jig was up. She let out a long, theatrical sigh, the kind that might have caused a cartoon steam cloud to appear above her head. Kyle, still dead to the world, snored softly. Good for him. He wouldn't have to face the music immediately.

With a final, melodramatic sigh that sounded suspiciously like a deflating balloon, Grace straightened her dress. The buttons, somehow, seemed to mock her fumbling efforts. Kyle's apartment suddenly felt like the stage for a very public, very embarrassing play. She had two choices: attempt a futile, ninja-like escape, or face the music head-on. Given her mother's internal clock and the fact that Grace had missed her usual 'snooze, groan, reluctantly wake up' period by a good hour, sneaking out was about as likely as finding a Starbucks on the ranch.

"Right," she murmured to the still-snoring Kyle, who remained blissfully unaware of the impending parental inquisition. "You snooze, you lose… or in this case, you snooze, I make coffee and wait for the parental apocalypse."

She took one last look around Kyle's room, making sure no incriminating evidence remained. It was surprisingly neat now, a stark contrast to the earlier tornado. Her 'stealth' skills, usually reserved for raiding the communal snack pantry at midnight, had been put to good use. With a tilt of her head, Grace decided coffee was the logical next step. A strong, black cup of courage. Or at least, a prop to clutch when Nicole arrived, eyes narrowed like a seasoned detective.

The light rap on the door, surprisingly gentle for the impending doom it heralded, made Grace jump. Her heart, already performing an Olympic-level drum solo, ratcheted up another notch. She took a fortifying gulp of the still-too-hot coffee, nearly scalding her tongue. Act natural, Grace. You're just... visiting. Very, very early.

She padded to the door, took a deep breath, and opened it a crack. Through the narrow gap, Nicole's familiar, kind face, framed by soft waves of silver hair, appeared. But her eyes, usually warm and trusting, held a glint that told Grace she wasn't buying any excuses before they were even uttered. "Grace? Darling, are you alright?" Nicole's voice was calm, almost too calm, like the eye of a hurricane. "I was a little worried when you weren't in your bed this morning." Her gaze flickered past Grace, subtly assessing the apartment's interior.

Grace pulled the door open wider, forcing a smile that felt painted on. She gripped her mug like a life raft. "Oh, Mom! Yeah, I'm fine! Just... uh... decided to get an early start on... uh... coffee. Kyle needed some." Her voice cracked on the last word. Smooth, Grace. Very smooth. Nicole stepped fully into the apartment, her eyes doing a slow, appraising sweep. "Well, since you're already brewing, darling, could you whip me up a cup too? Black, please. And don't mind me," she added.

Grace's brain went into overdrive. Coffee? For Mom? This is a trap. She's going to notice everything. Act normal. Brew the coffee. Don't spill it. Don't look guilty! "Oh, uh, sure, Mom! Coming right up!" She spun on her heel, nearly tripping over her own feet, and fumbled with the coffee pot, her hands trembling slightly as she poured. The clinking of porcelain against ceramic seemed deafening in the sudden silence of the apartment.

As Grace turned to the tiny kitchenette, Nicole's gaze sharpened on the floral pattern of Grace's dress. "My, that's a lovely dress, sweetheart," Nicole mused, her voice still perfectly serene. "Didn't you wear that last night?" The question hung in the air, light as a feather, but with the weight of a thousand judgments to Grace's suddenly hyperactive conscience. Grace nearly dropped the coffee pot. "This old thing? Oh, right, yeah, I did!

While Grace fussed with the coffee, Nicole slowly ran a hand over the suspiciously plumped cushions on the sofa. Her eyes then drifted over the meticulously cleared coffee table, the complete absence of Kyle's usual scattered gun parts or empty mugs. "And wow," Nicole continued, her voice laced with an almost theatrical surprise, "Kyle's really… tidied up, hasn't he? I don't think I've ever seen his apartment this organized. It's almost… sterile." She picked up a stray, non-descript coaster, examining it with a level of scrutiny usually reserved for antique artifacts.

Grace shoved the steaming mug of black coffee into her mother's hands, trying to distract her. "Yeah, he did!" she blurted out, a little too enthusiastically. "He's actually pretty neat when he tries! He said he wanted it to be, like, super nice for our date night. He really put in the effort, you know? So thoughtful. He even, uh, vacuumed!" She nodded vigorously, as if Kyle's hypothetical vacuuming was irrefutable proof of his innate tidiness. "The carpet was, like, perfectly patterned when I… uh… when I arrived this morning!" Great, Grace. Now you're just making things up.

Her words tumbled out in a rush, a waterfall of increasingly flimsy excuses. "And I, uh, I fell asleep here! On the couch, of course," she quickly corrected, pointing a finger at the very sofa Nicole was sitting on, as if to emphasize its strategic importance. "After, you know, we were playing Mortal Kombat so late.

"Oh, on the couch, you say?" Nicole purred, her voice dripping with an almost theatrical understanding. She met Grace's wide, blue eyes, which were darting around like trapped birds. "Well, honey, that couch does look remarkably inviting. And Kyle's apartment has never been quite so… pristine." She took a deliberate sip of the coffee Grace had handed her, her gaze never leaving her daughter's face. "You know, sometimes the truth is less about what you say, and more about what you don't say. And you, my sweet Grace, didn't technically lie."

Grace's shoulders sagged, a mix of relief and abject horror washing over her. Her mom knew. Of course, her mom knew. Nicole had probably seen through her flimsy excuses before Grace had even finished making them. The comedic irony was almost too much to bear. She offered a weak, unconvincing smile, her cheeks flushing crimson. "Right. Just… a very, very comfortable couch."

Just then, Kyle's bedroom door creaked open. He stepped out, looking surprisingly put-together for someone who had just woken up after a night of "Mortal Kombat". His hair was neatly combed, a clean, dark t-shirt hugged his frame, and jeans sat perfectly on his hips. He'd clearly had the wherewithal to get dressed. Nicole raised an eyebrow, a tiny smirk playing on her lips as she watched him approach.

"Good morning, Kyle," Nicole purred, her gaze sliding from Grace's crimson face to Kyle's slightly too-calm demeanor. Kyle stopped, a polite, almost too-bright smile fixed on his face. "Morning, Nicole. Grace. Sleep well?" He glanced at Grace, who was now staring intently at a strand of unraveled carpet. "Oh, splendid, thank you," Nicole replied, taking another slow, deliberate sip of her coffee. "Especially after that delightful 'Mortal Kombat' tournament you two had last night. Grace tells me you played quite vigorously." Her eyes twinkled, challenging him.

Kyle's smile didn't falter, but a faint flush crept up his neck. "Oh, yes! Very… vigorous. A real workout, that game. Lots of button-mashing, you know?" He gestured vaguely with one hand, as if demonstrating an invisible controller. "Some intense combos. Really gets the blood pumping." Grace let out a tiny, choked sound that might have been a whimper or a suppressed giggle, quickly covering it with a cough.

Nicole's smirk widened. "I'm sure it was. So," she paused, setting her coffee mug down with a deliberate clink on the small table beside her, her gaze sharpening, "How was your date with my daughter last night, Kyle? Beyond the button-mashing, that is." Kyle swallowed, his eyes darting quickly to Grace, who was now actively attempting to compress her body into a smaller, less noticeable form. "It was… delightful, Nicole. Truly. Grace is wonderful company.

We had a lovely dinner, then, as Grace mentioned, some spirited rounds of… of Mortal Kombat." He emphasized the game title a little too much. "She's quite good, actually."

Grace, meanwhile, was indeed trying to become one with the carpet fibers. Her internal monologue screamed abort, abort!. This was far worse than she'd imagined. Every fiber of her being urged her to flee, to somehow teleport directly into her room and hide under a pile of blankets until the sun set again. "Mom," she squeaked, "I think I'll just… go back to the house now. Check on Seth, maybe?"

Nicole, however, held up a hand. "Nonsense, sweetie. I just got here. Besides," she patted the empty spot on the sofa next to her, "I want to hear all about this 'vigorous' gaming session. I'm sure Kyle has more details he's just dying to share." Grace groaned internally. She knew that look. Her mom was enjoying this far too much, savoring every excruciating second of Kyle's discomfort. It felt like her mom was stalling, prolonging the agony, but for what?

Just as Kyle opened his mouth, presumably to offer another overly enthusiastic, vague description of pixelated violence, a polite but firm knock sounded on the open front door. "Come in!" Nicole called, her expression shifting instantly to one of warm welcome, though the mischievous glint in her eyes remained. Jennifer stepped into the living room, her usually bright smile amplified, a look in her eye that mirrored Nicole's.

She took in the scene: Jennifer's gaze settled on Nicole first, a quick, knowing flicker passing between them, before moving to Grace and then to Kyle, then returning to Nicole with a subtle eyebrow raise that sent goosebumps all over Grace's body. Grace, seeing Jennifer, felt a fresh wave of despair. Oh no. Not Aunt Jennifer! Her mom was one thing, but Aunt Jennifer was a whole other level of intelligence collection.

Jennifer, with a dramatic sigh that somehow conveyed both excitement and apology, crossed the room. She leaned over Grace, who was still attempting to become invisible, and gave her a warm kiss on the cheek. "Good morning, sweetie-pie," she purred, her voice a little too saccharine. "Did you sleep well?" Grace flinched, a full-body shudder. She reached up to touch her cheek, a donning realization washing over her. "Aunt Jennifer, you betrayed your niece with a kiss?" The nerve! The absolute, unmitigated gall! It was an ambush! A coordinated attack!

Jennifer pulled back, her smile widening into something entirely too knowing. "Betrayal? Oh, darling, no. Just... a very thorough morning greeting." Her eyes danced as she shared another quick, almost imperceptible glance with Nicole, who now had a small, satisfied smirk playing on her lips. The signal had been received, loud and clear.

Kyle, previously engrossed in his M-rated pixelated triumph, finally looked up, sensing the sudden shift in atmospheric pressure. He saw the gleam in the women's eyes, the way Grace was practically vibrating with mortification, and a slow, dawning horror spread across his face. He looked from Jen to Nicole, then to Grace, as if mentally calculating the odds of a tactical retreat. They were not in his favor.

"So," Nicole began, her voice deceptively gentle, "tell us all about your wonderful evening, Grace. And Kyle, of course." She gestured grandly at the couch, as if inviting them to share a thrilling tale of adventure. "Beyond the... Mortal Kombat, that is." Grace squeezed her eyes shut. Aunt Jennifer's kiss had obviously been a high-tech, bio-sensory sniff test, and she had failed spectacularly. Her face was burning. "It was... fine. We just... played games. And ate dinner." She tried to sound casual, but her voice cracked on "dinner."

Jennifer chimed in, "Oh, just dinner? And then?" She tapped a perfectly manicured finger to her chin, her gaze fixed on Kyle, who was now a vibrant shade of scarlet. "Did you perhaps... level up in any other areas, Kyle?" Kyle choked on air. "Uh... no! Just... you know. Talking. And... fatalities." He gestured vaguely at the TV, as if the blood and guts of the game were his only witnesses. He looked profoundly uncomfortable, a man caught between a rock and several very amused, very observant matriarchs.

Nicole leaned forward. "Grace, darling, are you quite sure there wasn't a... more personal victory to celebrate last night? Because your Aunt Jennifer, seems to think there might have been a rather... distinct aroma of celebration lingering." Grace squeezed her eyes shut again. She let out a small, defeated whimper. "We... we fell asleep on the couch," she mumbled, her eyes darting between Nicole's calm, analytical gaze and Jennifer's expectant, mischievous one. "And then... we went to bed. Together." The last word a whisper, a tiny, mortified admission.

31

Grace braced herself for the explosion, but it never came. Instead, Nicole's tranquil smile only widened. "Together, you say?" she mused, turning her gaze back to Kyle, who looked like a big stupid deer caught in the headlights of a very small, but very intelligent, and highly judgmental vehicle. "Kyle, darling, I must ask, was this a mutually enthusiastic endeavor? Or did our sweet Grace employ any... wiles to sway your judgment? Excessive alcohol, perhaps? Overly revealing attire? Or," Nicole paused, a theatrical finger tapping her chin, "dare I suggest, brute force?"

He remembered, with alarming clarity, the suspiciously convenient bottle of 'Cabernet' that Grace had insisted on sharing for their "romantic dinner," a bottle that seemed bottomless. He remembered his t-shirt, which had somehow ended up draped so casually over her naked body as they sprawled on the couch, the soft fabric doing nothing to hide the tantalizing curves beneath. And he most definitely remembered the surprising, almost alarming ease with which she had, indeed, pulled him onto her. Not to mention when she carried him to bed.

He swallowed hard, running a hand through his perpetually disheveled hair. "Nicole, it... Grace and I... what we did, we did together." He tried to meet her gaze, but his eyes kept darting to Grace, who offered him a tiny, knowing smirk that was utterly adorable and terrifying all at once. "We were both complicit." He managed to puff out his chest a little, trying to project an air of mature responsibility, rather than a man who had been charmingly outmaneuvered by a fifteen-year-old.

Nicole's expression softened, a subtle shift that only someone who knew her well would recognize as genuine relief. Her gaze lingered on Kyle for a moment longer, a silent acknowledgment of his response, before she gave a small, almost imperceptible nod. A true couple, indeed. They had stood together, even under the subtle pressure of her scrutiny.

Just as the tension in the space seemed to dissipate, a new, more vibrant energy burst forth. Jennifer, ever the instigator of delightful chaos, clapped her hands together, a mischievous twinkle dancing in her eyes. "Well, that's all very sweet and honorable, you two," she declared, her voice a playful lilt. "But how many times did you two manage to… copulate last night?"

Grace, who had just been absorbing Kyle's noble but slightly pathetic defense with an almost regal air, let out a dramatic, theatrical sigh. Her eyes rolled skyward, as if seeking divine intervention from the sheer audacity of Jennifer's query. It was a practiced, perfect roll — a masterpiece of teenage exasperation. Without a word, she spun on her heel, a flash of her usual sweetness replaced by a fleeting, almost imperceptible smirk towards Kyle, and then she was gone. The door to his room clicked shut behind her, leaving a pregnant silence in its wake.

Nicole, after a moment of silent contemplation, finally stirred. She offered Jennifer a look, then pushed herself up from the edge of the couch. Jennifer, ever agile, was already on her feet. They moved in tandem, two graceful predators, one playful, one observant, heading for the door. "Wait," Kyle blurted out, a sudden tremor of nervousness in his voice. He hadn't expected them to just... leave. Not after all that. He locked eyes with Nicole, his expression genuinely anxious. "Are you… are you mad?"

Nicole paused, her hand already on the doorknob. She turned, her expression unreadable at first, but then a faint, almost imperceptible smile touched her lips. "Mad?" she echoed, her voice calm, almost serene, as if discussing the weather. "No, Kyle. There's no reason for me to be mad." She tilted her head slightly, her gaze sharp. "Grace is a very capable young woman. If you hurt her, she'll just kill you herself."

As Nicole stepped into the stairwell of the apartment bunker, she saw a familiar figure heading down from the tunnel. Bonnie, her hair a bit disheveled, a faint blush still lingering on her cheeks, was quietly making her way towards the stairs. Her eyes widened slightly as she spotted Nicole. "Bonnie, dear," Nicole said, her voice gentle. "Are you heading home?" Bonnie nodded, her gaze flickering nervously to Jennifer, then back to Nicole. "Yes, Mrs. Nicole."

"Perfect timing," Nicole chirped, falling into step beside her. Jennifer, ever intuitive, gave Nicole a knowing glance and continued toward the main house. "How about I walk you back? It's no trouble at all." Bonnie's eyes darted away. "Oh, you don't have to, Mrs. Nicole. I know the way." Nicole chuckled softly, a warm, maternal sound. "Nonsense, and besides," she leaned in, lowering her voice just a fraction,

"I think your dad might be a little more lenient about you seeing Seth, if he knows I'm involved. You know, a parent thing." She offered Bonnie a sweet, reassuring smile. "It always helps when it looks like the adults are on the same page, even when we're just... chaperoning a walk home."

Bonnie's eyes widened again, and a small, hopeful smile touched her lips. "Okay," she murmured, a little shyly. "Thank you, Mrs. Nicole." "Bonnie, dear," Nicole began, her voice a comforting murmur that bounced off the concrete walls. "There's really no need to be shy around me, you know. Besides, you're practically family already. You two make quite the adorable pair, and if I'm not mistaken, it won't be long before you'll be my daughter-in-law." Nicole's words were delivered with such an open, loving sincerity that it took the sting out of Bonnie's earlier embarrassment, replacing it with a fresh wave of blush.

Bonnie's head snapped up, her eyes wide with surprise, then flickered down to her sneakers, a small, shy smile finally gracing her lips. "D-daughter-in-law?" she whispered, the idea seemingly too grand, too grown-up, for her age. Nicole chuckled, a warm sound that echoed pleasantly in the quiet hall. "Oh, yes! Seth has chosen you, and that's usually how it goes around here. When a boy knows what he wants, and the girl feels the same way, we just let nature take its course. Of course, there's still plenty of time for you to just be a kid, too. No rush on the grown-up stuff, but it's good to know where things are heading." She patted Bonnie lightly on the shoulder. "And when you are grown and settled in, you'll be joining a very special group here. It's truly a sisterhood."

Bonnie looked up again, captivated. "A sisterhood?" "Oh, yes!" Nicole's eyes sparkled. "Look around you, sweet pea. When you and Seth are older, you'll be one of us. We are all deeply connected. It's not just about holidays and family dinners, it's about sharing a life, a purpose. It's about building something, together, that's bigger than any one of us could imagine alone."

Bonnie absorbed her words. "It just… it feels really grown up, Mrs. Nicole. More than just, you know, kids liking each other. Like… it's serious." She said, her voice dropping. "Like it's not really a game at all." A soft, knowing smile played on Nicole's lips. "Because it isn't, Bonnie. Not anymore. This isn't the world we used to live in, where relationships were just a part of your life, something you fit in between work, hobbies, and social plans. Here, relationships are your life. They're the foundation everything else is built on."

"I guess so. It just… it sounded a little scary at first." She paused, then blurted out, "I was worried I'd have, like, so many moms bossing me around all the time." Her eyes widened, as if the thought had truly haunted her. "Like, 'Bonnie, did you do your chores?' from five different people, or 'Bonnie, you can't wear that!' or 'Bonnie, you finish your vegetables!'" She mimed a stern finger wagging, her small face comically serious. "It sounded like a lot of rules, and a lot of… moms."

Nicole chuckled, a warm, reassuring sound. "Oh, Bonnie. Is that what you thought?" "Well, yeah!" Bonnie nodded earnestly. "I mean, there are lots of moms here." Bonnie gestured vaguely with her hand. "And I just thought, if Seth and I... you know, if we got married like he talks about, then I'd be part of all that, and everyone would be my mom. And that's just a lot of moms." "And what did Seth say about that?" Nicole prompted, her smile softening with amusement.

Bonnie's cheeks flushed slightly. "He said... he said it's not like that. He said it's more like... a team. He said grown-ups just... help each other. And you get to decide things for yourself, too." She looked up, hopeful. "Is that true?" "Seth is a very wise young man, isn't he?" Nicole beamed, clearly proud of her observant son. "He's absolutely right, Bonnie. It's a team, a very big, loving team. And no, we don't 'boss' anyone around. We empower each other. Especially our girls." Nicole leaned forward slightly, her gaze earnest. "We believe in raising our daughters to be women, Bonnie. Not just older versions of themselves, or perpetual 'daughters' who never quite grow up. We want you and the others to blossom into strong, capable, independent women who know their worth and contribute to the family and this community in your own unique ways."

Bonnie wrinkled her nose, processing this. "So, like, I get to be a grown-up lady who helps out, instead of just a kid who gets told what to do?" Nicole's smile widened. "Precisely, sweet pea. And here's the best part: you've already been training for it. Every single day since you got here."

Bonnie's eyes, wide with a newfound understanding, drifted down to her hip. There, nestled securely in its holster, was her P365. It wasn't just a weight on her belt; it was a symbol she hadn't quite deciphered until now. It wasn't a toy, not a prop for make-believe adventures with Seth. It was real. It was a tool, a responsibility, given to her by the very adults she'd initially feared might "boss her around." They hadn't just given it to her; they'd taught her how to use it, how to clean it, when not to use it. They trusted her with it.

A small, smile touched her lips, a dawning realization that smoothed away the earlier wrinkle of her nose. She wasn't just a kid here, a tag-along member of David's ever-expanding family. She was part of the team. A grown-up lady who helps out. The thought was both daunting and exhilarating. Seth was right, as usual. It wasn't about being told what to do; it was about learning how to do.

As Nicole and Bonnie reached the door, Eric, who had just emerged, probably on his way to the armory, stopped short. His eyes brightened as he saw Nicole. A genuine, appreciative smile touched his lips. "Nicole, good morning," Eric greeted, a quiet warmth in his voice. He glanced at Bonnie, then back at Nicole, a silent message of gratitude passing between the two adults. "Thanks for... looking out for her."

Nicole returned a sweet smile. "Of course, Eric. Bonnie's a smart girl. We were just having a chat about responsibilities. She's really coming into her own." Bonnie, still buzzing from her "responsibility" revelation, practically skipped back to her room. The earlier encounter with Nicole had cemented something profound in her mind. The idea of helping now held a certain allure, like a secret level unlocked in a video game.

Chapter 15:

The Pig Pen Project

Inside the classroom, Grace wrapped up her lesson on different forms of government. "So, to recap," she said, adjusting the whiteboard, "democracy is when everyone gets a say, a republic has elected officials, and... well, what's a benevolent dictatorship, Bonnie?" Bonnie blinked. "Uh... it's when someone really nice is in charge?" A few giggles rippled through the classroom. Grace smiled patiently. "Close. It's when one person has absolute power, but they use it for the good of the people, like Daddy."

Clarence scoffed from his usual corner seat, where he often held court or complained, today it was the latter. "Benevolent, my foot! He tries to control my diet. I want steak and potatoes! Not all this rabbit food they keep giving me!" Grace retorted without missing a beat, her tone sweet but laced with steel, "Summer and Kayla control your diet, Clarence, because they're trying to keep you from spontaneously combusting from too much bacon grease. And if you are so eager to end your life early, just meet me behind the barn later, and I promise to make it quick."

Meanwhile, over in the nursery, Kathy was attempting to wrangle Poppy, who was careening around the room like a tiny, babbling tornado. Taylor watched with a fond smile as Lucas watched from his tiny recliner. "She's... energetic," Kathy said, wiping sweat from her brow. "And talkative! She called me 'Aunty Kathy' this morning." "They learn fast," Taylor said, patting Lucas's tummy. "It's a bit freaky, actually. Now I know how Nicole felt with the twins."

Scott, the Butcher, paced with a furrowed brow in the main living room as Aidan watched, Tiffany sitting on the opposite couch. "Aidan, I need your brain on something," Scott began, gesturing vaguely towards the kitchen. "The freeze-dried supply is... well, it's not insufficient yet, not by a long shot, but it's not fresh. And we've got a lot of mouths to feed. I'm thinking pigs. Wild pigs. There's got to be plenty out there, right? Especially with no one else around to hunt them."

Aidan nodded slowly. "You're not wrong, Scott. Texas has always had a significant wild hog population, and without traditional hunting pressure, they'd certainly be thriving. The sheer number of them out there is probably staggering right now. And, granted, they grow fast, reproduce quickly, and provide a lot of meat." He leaned forward, his tone shifting. "However, there's a significant downside to hunting wild game in our current situation, particularly pigs." Scott stopped pacing. "Downside? Like what, they're tough to catch?"

Aidan shook his head. "No, Scott, not that. The risk of disease. In a world without functioning public health services, without proper veterinary care, and with so many people dying, bringing in wild animals is incredibly risky. Wild pigs are already notorious carriers of various parasites and diseases, like brucellosis, trichinosis, pseudorabies... even less common things that could spread and wipe out our existing livestock, or worse, make people incredibly sick. What's a minor ailment for a wild animal could be catastrophic for us without access to proper medical intervention."

Scott's brow furrowed deeper. "So, we just... don't get fresh pork? Ever?" He looked genuinely crestfallen. Aidan offered a sympathetic half-smile. "Not from the wild, not safely. But there's a better, more controlled way. Instead of hunting them, we should be catching and breeding them. We capture healthy specimens, young ones, if possible, and then... well, Tiffany, you were just talking about it." He gestured to her.

Tiffany, elegant and poised, chimed in. "Exactly. If we bring in any wild animals, whether for breeding or consumption, we'd have to quarantine them for several months. At least three, possibly six, depending on what we're looking for. It's the only way to ensure they aren't carrying anything that could compromise the health of our existing animals or, far more critically, our people."

Scott's shoulders slumped. "Quarantine? For months? Where would we even put them? We can't just tie a pig to a tree in the yard, not with how the weather is." "No, of course not," Tiffany said calmly. "We'd need a secure, separate enclosure. Something far enough from the barn and the main house to prevent any cross-contamination. It would need its own feeding and watering stations, and a dedicated team for their care and observation. We'd be watching for any signs of illness, anything unusual. It's a significant undertaking."

Aidan added, "Think of it as an investment. We need to be absolutely certain before we introduce anything new to

42

our ecosystem here. Breeding them ourselves gives us control, allows for proper vaccination if we can manage it, and ensures a sustained, healthy supply without the constant risk assessment of wild hunts." Scott sighed, running both hands through his hair this time, clearly processing the implications. "So, no spontaneous bacon. Just... planned, strategic, heavily observed, six-month-wait bacon."

Tiffany, ever the picture of serene practicality, offered a small smile. "Think of it as an exercise in delayed gratification, dear. No one wants to introduce a vector of disease into our carefully cultivated little paradise. The last thing we need is a porcine pandemic wiping out our future dinner." Aidan nodded. "Exactly. And to that end, we need to get started on the infrastructure sooner rather than later. I'll go track down Junior after this and talk to him about getting a crew together. We'll need to dig out a significant foundation for that quarantine building, somewhere to the east, closer to the range, but nestled against the hillside." He paused, looking directly at Scott. "It's not just a hole, Scott. It's gotta be secure, deep enough for foundations, and then reinforced."

Scott nodded slowly. "Right. Junior and his nocturnal earth-moving specialists. Makes sense. But that ground out there... it's a pain. Rocky as hell in places. I tried to sink a fence post once and nearly broke my arms. Which reminds me. I'll talk to Mark. We might need to blast the ground in some spots, especially if we hit solid rock. Faster than pickaxes in this heat, and honestly, a lot more satisfying." Tiffany chuckled. "Just make sure Mark coordinates with

Junior, then. We don't want any accidental land-clearing projects impacting the range, or worse, the bunkers."

Aidan stood up, stretching his arms above his head. "Will do. Strategic demolition for strategic bacon. Quite the operation, isn't it?" He walked over to one of the French doors, peering out at the late afternoon sun beginning its slow descent. Just then, the soft creak of the garage door announced an arrival. Grace emerged onto the main living level. "Hey, Aunt Tiff, Uncle Scott, Aidan," she greeted, her voice a soft, melodic hum. "Everything okay? I heard something about... bacon?"

Aidan turned, a warm smile gracing his features. "Hey, Grace. Everything's fine. Just planning for future bacon, which, it turns out, is a mission, in and of itself. Listen, I need your help with something. Could you do me a favor and go fetch Kyle? I need to have a chat with him, and I figured you'd be the fastest way to get him here to the main house." Grace's cheeks flushed a faint pink. "Sure, Aidan. I'll go get him." She turned and, with a purposeful stride, headed outside, towards the work shed.

Grace entered the shed, her eyes immediately drawn to Marvin. He was meticulously working on a block of metal, his brow furrowed in concentration. She recognized the pattern forming; it was going to be a Damascus blade. She knew Marvin wasn't a natural bladesmith like Kyle, but his dedication was admirable. "Hey, Marvin," Grace said softly, approaching the workbench.

Marvin looked up, startled. "Grace! Hey. Didn't hear you come in. What's up?" He wiped his hands on a rag, a sheepish grin spreading across his face. "Just trying my hand at smithing. Not sure it's going to work out, but Kyle's a good teacher." Grace leaned closer, genuinely impressed. "Wow, that's... that's really cool, Marvin. I know it's hard, but you're really going for it. Is there a reason why you decided to start making Damascus Blades?"

Marvin shrugged, "Don't really have a project right now, plus I figured this was a good way to get in some practice. Plus, the idea of being a black blacksmith is hilarious. Like a perpetual inside joke." She paused, marveling at his dedication and... unusual sense of humor. "That's really awesome, Marvin. I didn't know you were so into learning new things." Marvin chuckled. "Well, there's a lot you don't know about me, Grace. But, uh, I'm guessing you didn't come out here just to admire my... skills."

Grace blushed, suddenly remembering her errand. "Oh, right! Aidan wants to see Kyle. He said it was important." She looked around the cluttered workshop, finally spotting Kyle near the back, meticulously sorting and labeling his scrap metal. He seemed to have a system, but to the untrained eye, it just looked like a mountain of rusty junk. "Kyle!" she called out, her voice carrying a touch of affection that made Marvin raise an eyebrow.

Kyle looked up, a smile instantly gracing his face as he saw Grace. He tossed the metal he was holding back into its designated pile, "Usable Edges," apparently, and strode towards her. Before Marvin could even blink, Grace launched herself into Kyle's arms, wrapping her legs around his waist. She pulled him into a deep, passionate kiss that left no room for doubt about their... relationship. Marvin coughed awkwardly, looking away.

Finally, Grace broke the kiss, a slightly breathless, blissfully happy smile on her face. She hopped down, adjusting her clothes. "Hey, babe. Aidan wants to talk to you. Something about strategic bacon." Grace skipped ahead, her hand intertwined with his, humming a tuneless melody. "Strategic bacon, huh?" Kyle chuckled, shaking his head. "That sounds like something only Aidan could come up with."

"He's been talking with Scott about sustainable pork production," Grace replied, rolling her eyes playfully. "Apparently, our current bacon supply is 'unsustainable' and we need to diversify our... pig portfolio?" Kyle laughed. "Diversify the pig portfolio? Is he planning on taking the pigs to Wall Street?"

Kyle and Grace entered the living room, hand-in-hand, radiating a smug contentment that nauseated outsiders. Aidan grinned as he saw them. Scott, lounging on the sofa, just grunted. Tiffany, however, raised an eyebrow. "Alright you two, save it for later. There's strategic bacon to discuss." Kyle cleared his throat, trying to look less like a teenager caught making out in the back of a car. "So, strategic bacon, huh? What's this all about, Aidan?"

Aidan smoothed down his perpetually rumpled t-shirt. "Alright, so Scott here's been hankering for some fresh pork, right? But just hunting wild pigs? That comes with too many risks. We need a long-term solution. That's where you two come in. I need you and Grace to go with Scott and Mike to go capture several young wild pigs. Ideal breeding stock." "Capture?" Kyle repeated, his eyebrow arching. "Just walk up and ask them nicely?" Scott snorted. "I was thinkin' more along the lines of… pig-napping."

Grace spoke up. "Tiffany suggested quarantining any wild animals for a while before introducing them. Smart, right? Don't wanna contaminate our livestock." Aidan nodded approvingly. "Precisely! So, we need a holding area. Safe, secure, and… well, pig-proof." Tiffany added, "And humane, Aidan. Remember, these are our future bacon makers, not convicts." Kyle rubbed his chin thoughtfully. "So, capture pigs, quarantine pigs… where are we putting these guys?"

Aidan clapped his hands together. "Ah, that's the thing! I was thinking of building onto the property, up to the Northeast, into the hillside. It'll be a bit of a bunker-esque structure… Very stout, made of reinforced concrete to start. It'll serve as a perfect quarantine pen and it would have proper drainage… easy to sanitize once it's no longer needed. " "So… a pig bunker?" Kyle deadpanned. "A strategic bacon bunker!" Aidan corrected, grinning. "Think of it as an investment in our future breakfast. It would allow us to control light and airflow and everything else like that…"

Scott grumbled, "Sounds like a whole lot of work for some pork chops." Tiffany swatted him lightly on the arm. "Hush, Scott. We need to think long-term. Besides, the bunker idea has potential." Kyle leaned back in his chair, a discerning in his eye. "You know, that concrete work… it got me thinking. We've been patching up tools and weapons using the forge in the workshop. It's small and cramped, frankly dangerous, and not at all efficient. Building that bunker... we could build it big enough to convert it into a proper Smithy."

Suddenly, Grace, who'd been unusually quiet, piped up. "If it was bigger, maybe we could even make it big enough for a proper machine shop too!" Her eyes sparkled with enthusiasm, and Aidan grinned. "Absolutely! We could put a lathe and all sorts of equipment in there. Imagine the possibilities!" Aidan was practically bouncing in his seat. Scott sighed dramatically. "Right, so instead of a pig pen, we're building a goddamn industrial complex for swine?"

Kyle chuckled correcting him, "Not exactly, Scott. We build the building for the pig quarantine now, but big enough to easily convert into a Smithy later. Think of it as future-proofing." Aidan clapped his hands together. "Kyle, that's brilliant! Future-proofing! Exactly! Okay, everyone, listen up. Kyle, grab some paper, sketch out a basic floor plan. Think about workflow, ventilation, layout, everything. Grace, you work with him on the machine shop aspect. Once it's done, I'll have everyone take a look at it and get a proper blueprint drafted?"

Meanwhile, oblivious to the flurry of activity surrounding pig pens and future machine shops, Junior was waking up. A morning sunrise, filtered weakly through the window, barely illuminating the scene. He stretched, groaning quietly, his body a symphony of aches and pleasant exhaustion. Three women were tangled around him, a human pretzel of limbs and soft, naked skin. Riley, on his right, her red hair splayed across his chest, her eternity collar cool against his skin. Olivia, on his left, her serene face nestled against his shoulder. And Emma, the most petite of the three, was spooning Riley, her arm possessively draped across her waist.

Riley stirred first, her eyes fluttering open. "Mmm, mornin', handsome," she mumbled, her voice thick with sleep. She leaned up, pressing a sloppy, morning-breath kiss to his lips. Before Junior could reciprocate, Olivia's eyes opened, a soft smile gracing her lips. "Good morning, love," she purred, mirroring Riley's action with a gentler, more deliberate kiss. "Alright, alright, break it up," Junior chuckled, pushing them away playfully. "Coffee. Shower. World domination. Priorities, ladies!"

Olivia untangled herself smoothly. "Coffee is on the way, sir," she said, already heading towards the kitchenette, her bare feet padding softly on the carpet. "What's on the menu for 'world domination' today?" Junior stretched, his muscles popping in the dim light. "Debrief with Aidan, we'll see what he says. After that...patrol, maybe some weapons maintenance. You know, the usual apocalyptic fun."

Without a word, Emma slid from the bed, her naked form moving with a quiet grace born of comfortable resignation. She padded into the adjoining kitchenette, the linoleum cool beneath her feet. Back in the bedroom, Junior stretched. "Riley," he rumbled, his voice low. "Still with us?" A muffled groan came from the tangle of sheets. "Five more millennia." Junior chuckled. He pointed a finger toward the bathroom. "Shower time. Riley, wanna scrub my back?"

The effect was instantaneous. Riley shot up in bed, her red hair a wild mess, her eyes wide and practically vibrating with enthusiasm. "Do you even have to ask?" She scrambled off the bed, a blur of pale skin and pure energy. "Come on, big guy!" she chirped, grabbing his hand and practically dragging him toward the bathroom door. " I have some very specific, deep-cleaning techniques in mind!"

Meanwhile, in the kitchenette, Olivia was a picture of serene competence. Dressed in nothing but her own collar, she expertly cracked eggs with one hand into a hot, buttered pan while simultaneously turning beef sausage patties with a fork. "Emma, honey," Olivia said. "Can you make some cinnamon toast? We haven't had that in a while."

Emma nodded eagerly, her whole face lighting up. "Oh, I love cinnamon toast," she said, her voice soft as she unwrapped a loaf of fresh-baked bread. She began meticulously buttering slices, her movements precise. "Ooh, Olivia," she added, her brow furrowed in genuine concern as a drop of hot grease spat from the sausage pan, landing perilously close. "Be careful! The sausage is spitting. You might want to put on an apron so you don't splash hot oil on your tits." Olivia glanced down at her chest and chuckled. "A valid point, sweetie. Thank you," Olivia chuckled, her eyes crinkling at the corners. She didn't reach for an apron, instead just taking a small step back from the spitting pan. "I think he likes it when we don't wear clothes."

Emma giggled, a light, airy sound. She was meticulously arranging the buttered bread slices on a baking sheet. "He does," she agreed with reverent softness. "But he likes your skin more." She sprinkled a generous layer of cinnamon and sugar over the bread, her movements as delicate as if she were dusting a butterfly's wings.

Meanwhile, the bathroom was a cloud of steam. The rhythmic slap of skin against skin had ceased, replaced by the steady drumming of hot water against the tiled shower wall. Riley leaned her forehead against the cool, wet tiles, her breath coming in ragged, satisfied gasps. The water sluiced over her back, tracing paths down her spine and over the faint red marks blooming on her skin. Behind her, Junior shut off the water, the sudden silence amplifying the sound of their breathing.

He rested his chin on her shoulder, his large hand splayed possessively across her abdomen. "Good start to the day," he rumbled, his voice a low vibration against her ear. Riley twisted her head slightly, a sarcastic smirk playing on her lips. "You say that every night. One of these days you're going to have to come up with new material."

He chuckled, a deep, easy sound. "Don't fix what isn't broken." He gave her a final squeeze before stepping out of the shower, grabbing a towel. Riley followed, her legs nearly buckling under her. As Junior dried himself off, she grabbed her towel and went straight to the bedroom. After drying off, she pulled on a pair of black leggings and a faded blue t-shirt that hugged her form.

Junior watched her, amused. "Putting on your armor already?" "It's called tactical layering," she shot back, pulling her damp hair back into a messy knot. "Last time, Olivia's sausage spat at me. I'm not taking a direct hit from rogue breakfast grease for anyone. Plus, if I don't put something on, I'll have to shower again."

The scent of cinnamon and sausage wafted from the apartment's kitchenette, a sweet and inviting aroma that promised a pleasant start to their "morning." Junior, still damp from the shower with a single white towel knotted low on his hips, followed the scent from the bedroom. He stepped over the threshold into the living space, his bare feet silent on the carpet. Riley, now fully clad in her "tactical" leggings and t-shirt, followed a few paces behind him, observing the scene with a wry detachment.

In the kitchen, Olivia stood at the stove, her back to them. Her weight shifted on one leg as she finished with the eggs. A plate piled high with perfectly cooked sausage patties sat on the counter beside her. Everything about her posture screamed 'fuck me', from the curved line of her spine to the bend in her knee, just above her little foot, perched on her tippy toes.

The moment Junior's bare foot crossed the line from the carpeted living area to the cool linoleum of the kitchenette, Emma's head snapped up from where she'd been setting the table. Her movements were fluid and practiced, completely devoid of hesitation. She turned, and in one smooth motion, removed her apron and dropped to her knees before him. Her small hands finding the knot of his towel, and with a deft tug, it loosened and fell away, pooling in a soft white heap on the floor.

Junior let out a low chuckle as she took his cock down her throat. The sound a deep rumble in his chest that vibrated down into Emma's very core. He didn't move to stop her, but his hand came to rest gently on the back of her head, his fingers threading through her hair. It wasn't a gesture of command, but one of casual, possessive affection. His gaze flicked from the top of Emma's devoted head to Riley, who was still posed dramatically in the doorway.

"And the show starts early tonight, folks," Riley announced with the flair of a ringmaster. "Someone's eager for her performance review." Junior's lips curved into a smirk. "She's always aiming for Employee of the Month," he retorted, his voice laced with amusement. "Points for initiative."

Olivia, ever the picture of graceful efficiency, navigated the scene as if stepping over a devoted, kneeling wife was the most normal thing for them. She placed the platters of sizzling sausage and fried eggs on the small dining table before returning to give Junior a lingering kiss on the cheek. Her own naked body brushed against his side, a brief, warm press of skin. "Don't let her distract you too long," she murmured, her breath ghosting against his ear. "Food's ready." Her eyes, sparkling.

Emma, oblivious to the banter, continued with a single-minded focus that was both awe-inspiring and slightly terrifying. Her entire world had narrowed to this one, singular act of worship. For her, this wasn't a performance; it was breathing. Junior let her continue for another moment, enjoying the absolute surrender, the sheer force of her devotion. Finally, with a soft sigh, his hand on her head applied the slightest pressure, a silent command. "Alright, little bird," he said, his voice soft but firm. "Come up for air."

Instantly, Emma obeyed. She released him with a soft sound of reluctance and looked up at him, her eyes wide and adoring, lips glistening. There was no shame, no hesitation, only the pure, unfiltered question of whether she had pleased him. He leaned down and captured her mouth in a deep, rewarding kiss. "Good girl," he praised, the two words lighting her up from the inside. He helped her to her feet, his hands on her waist. He then gave her a gentle nudge toward the table. "Now, breakfast. We've got a long night ahead of us."

Riley was already seated at the small dining table, a piece of cinnamon toast held delicately in her fingers. She watched Emma get settled with a wry, sarcastic arch of her eyebrow. "Right," she said, her voice dry as a Texas summer. "Strategic fuel consumption. The sexiest kind of pre-shift pillow talk."

Olivia, unfazed, poured them all glasses of orange juice, her bare tits nearly dipping into her toast. "It's a valid logistical concern, Riley. Better to discuss it now than when we're a hundred miles out and running on fumes." She sat down, her posture perfect even as she reached for a sausage patty.

Junior took a hearty bite of his eggs, chewing thoughtfully before swallowing. He looked from Olivia's earnest face to Riley's smirk. "Dad's not wrong to be concerned," he began. "Forty-thousand gallons is a lot to just let go bad. But we honestly anticipated using more." He gestured with his fork. "We've been favoring the propane-converted trucks for a reason. They're simpler to maintain, the fuel source is more stable long-term, and considerably more cargo space. The gasoline is for specific, high-speed, low-drag missions where we might need the performance of Dad's sedan or Elena's car, like an escort or scouting mission. We just haven't had many of those lately."

Emma listened, but not to the words. She was listening to the cadence of Junior's voice, watching the way his throat moved when he spoke, the focused look in his eyes. To her, the topic was irrelevant; the man speaking was everything. She ate her own breakfast diligently, her plate clean long before anyone else's. "So what's the plan, then?" Olivia asked. "Just let it expire?"

"Nah," Junior shook his head, a ghost of a smile playing on his lips. "We give it another year. If we're still sitting on a massive surplus by next summer, we just start running the gasoline generators instead of propane. We'll burn through what's left in a few months, top off the battery banks, and call it a win. Free power, problem solved." "Junior?" Emma asked softly. "Yeah, little bird?" She took a small breath, her gaze unwavering. "I finished my breakfast." She paused for a beat. "Can I finish sucking your dick now, please?"

The question hung in the air, completely devoid of the shock it would have carried anywhere else on Earth. Riley sputtered into her orange juice, a laugh catching in her throat. "Subtlety," she coughed, wiping her mouth with the back of her hand, "thy name is Emma." Olivia simply smiled, a serene, knowing expression on her face as she looked at Junior. "See? I told you not to let her get distracted for too long."

Junior gave Emma a simple, decisive nod, his expression unreadable for a moment before he turned his attention back to the other two women at the table. "Anyway," he said, clearing his throat as Emma dutifully retrieved a small, padded kneeling mat from beside her chair. "The point is, the plan is adaptable." Emma disappeared beneath the table. The only sounds were the soft scrape of her mat on the floor and the faint the wet slurps of her mouth sliding over his cock.

Riley propped her chin on her hand, a devilish look in her eyes. "Adaptable is good. You have to be ready for... unforeseen circumstances that might pop up." She took a long, slow sip of her orange juice, her gaze fixed on Junior's face, waiting for the slightest crack in his composure.

Riley chewed on a piece of cinnamon toast, her eyes dancing with unconcealed mischief. She glanced at Olivia and mouths the word "stabilization" before taking a noisy gulp of her orange juice. "So you're just... keeping the engine primed?" she asked, her voice laced with a feigned innocence that fools no one. "Making sure all the... moving parts... stay lubricated?"

A muscle in Junior's jaw clenched for a split second, the only outward sign that he's being affected. He set his coffee cup down with deliberate care. "It's about maintaining operational readiness, Riley. You know that. We have contingencies for our contingencies. Having Dad second-guess our fuel management is just... Tuesday." Olivia smiled gently. "David doesn't second-guess, dear. He tests. He wants to know that you've thought it all through." She looked at Junior, her gaze soft but perceptive. "And it's clear that you have. You're handling your assets with remarkable focus."

The word "assets" hung in the air, thick with double meaning. Junior let out a slow, controlled breath as a muffled sound of pure, unadulterated bliss emanated from beneath the table. He closed his eyes for a long moment, his powerful frame going utterly still. After a long, silent calm, he opened his eyes, his focus returning like a camera lens snapping into sharpness. "We manage," he said, slightly winded. He looked from Riley's smirk to Olivia's knowing smile. "Alright. I think we've covered logistics for now," he said, placing a large hand flat on the table.

A few moments later, Emma emerged, her hair slightly mussed, her cheeks flushed, and her eyes shining with a look of profound devotion. She rose gracefully, wiping the corner of her mouth. After stowing her kneeling mat, she then went to the bathroom, turning on the shower. After watching Emma's graceful exit, Olivia tilted her head, her dark eyes sparkling with a familiar, intelligent mischief. She didn't even bother to lower her voice. "So," she began, her tone as casual as if she were asking him to pass the salt. "Are you going to fuck me now, or what?" Riley jumped up. "I'll clear the table."

Chapter 16:

The Callie Fornication Girl

In the main living room, a farcical debate was still brewing, fueled by Scott's insatiable desire for fresh pork. The door swung open, and Junior sauntered in, a picture of casual confidence. He was dressed in his usual uniform of tactical pants and a black t-shirt. His signature X-Ten rested comfortably on his hip. He bore a lazy smile that suggested a very satisfying morning. "Sorry I'm late," Junior drawled. "Had a… productive morning." He let the implication hang in the air, earning a snort from Kyle, who was trying to suppress a grin.

"Glad you could join us, Junior," Aidan said, a hint of exasperation lacing his voice. "We're discussing Scott's pig obsession." "Pigs, huh?" Junior's eyes lit up. "A living bacon farm." He looked at Scott. "What's the plan?" Scott, emboldened by Junior's arrival, launched back into his argument. "I just want some fresh pork! We can hunt them down, bring 'em back, and bam! Instant pig roast! But your brother wants to breed them, which is cool, but will slow down the process."

Aidan sighed. "Junior, I need your team to start prepping the site for new construction. We'll build a smithy for Kyle, but for now, use it as a holding area for our quarantine. I want to build it into the hillside, northwest of here." Junior snapped his fingers. "No problem. We can start marking and clearing the area today." He looked at Grace. "Grace, are you and Kyle involved in the pig collection or the smithy construction?"

Grace, piped up, "We'll go with Scott and Mike to get the pigs. Kyle can start on the smithy's blueprints in the meantime. He has some ideas he wants to put on paper." Kyle nodded in agreement. "Yeah, I'll sketch it out. Maybe some reinforced sections, good ventilation, the works. Gotta make it apocalypse-proof, you know?" Aidan rubbed his temples. "Okay, so the Smithy/pig-jail is going to be built against the hillside, to the Northeast.

Speaking of hillside, I spoke with Mark, and he's going to try and acquire explosives to help with the excavation." Junior whistled softly. "Now that's what I'm talking about, let's get this party started. Some explosives will definitely make this building project go faster. But for now, me and my team will begin gathering building supplies."

Later, downstairs, Junior leaned against a countertop, a half-eaten protein bar in his hand. His usual smirk, tempered by a focused intensity. Emma, Olivia, and Riley sitting closest to him while the rest of the night shift, Caleb, Darrel, Callie, Kathy, Noah, Reagan, and Sophia, were sprawled around the table eating their breakfast, some looking more awake than others. Andrew and Susan, meanwhile, sat quietly on chairs by the door.

"Alright, listen up," Junior began, his voice cutting through the low murmur of conversation. "Day shift dropped a project on us. Aidan wants a new building. A smithy for Kyle and a temporary pig-jail, all rolled into one. Built into the hillside, Northeast side of the property." A wave of groans washed over the room. Noah let out a particularly dramatic sigh. "Hillside? Seriously? That's gonna be a bitch." He ran a hand over his head, his face etched with exhaustion. "Couldn't he just, I don't know, ask the pigs nicely to stay put?"

Junior cracked a wider grin, tossing the remnants of his protein bar in the trash. "Tell me about it, Noah. I'd rather be charming some wild hogs with sweet nothings than hauling concrete. But," he drew out the word, his eyes twinkling, "think about the bacon. Think about the future breakfast sammies. Think about the glory!" He punctuated 'glory' with a fist pump, which earned him a few tired chuckles. Emma leaned forward, her brow furrowed with concern. "The hillside, though? That sounds... complicated. Are we talking dynamite?"

"Aidan's working on that," Junior replied, shooting a playful glare at Emma. "Our primary role for now is surveying the site and resource acquisition. Plus, Aidan wants it integrated into the terrain, you know? All fancy and shit." Riley snorted. "Aidan? Fancy? That's a new one. I thought he only cared about engines and Alissa." "Look, Aidan's got a ranch to manage, okay? And this pig-jail, as glamorous as it sounds, is temporary. It's a stopgap measure. Once we've quarantined the bugs out of them, the pigs will move to a proper pen." He paused, running a hand through his hair. "Besides," he added with a mischievous grin, "a smithy integrated into the hillside? Sounds badass."

Darrel, his brow furrowed in thought, piped up, "Okay, okay, bacon-fueled badassery. I'm in. But since you said this pig pen is temporary, are we thinking of adding onto the barn once we get the breeding thing down? I mean, gotta plan ahead, right? Don't want to be chasing piglets all over the ranch." He swirled the ice in his glass of iced tea.

Junior nodded, appreciating Darrel's foresight. "Good question, Darrel. That's something we need to discuss. Long-term, yeah, expanding the barn is the most logical option. Maybe even a separate, dedicated piggery. Less mooing and squawking to spook the swine if we keep them separated." Junior sighed. "Okay, people, let's get back on track. The bacon-shaped prize awaits! We'll save the building upgrades for later. For now, here's the plan. I want a survey team to head out to the Northeast hillside, Aidan can give you the exact coordinates and mark the area. We need to know the dimensions, the terrain, and any potential obstacles. Riley, Emma, Reagan, and Callie you're on the survey team. Get your gear ready. "The rest of us," he continued, clapping his hands together, "will focus on initial scouting and resource gathering.

As the four women went outside, Reagan piped up with a thoughtful expression. "So, Emma... you guys are all, y'know, close with Junior, right? I was just wondering...does... uh... Junior's... well, does his sperm ever make you feel better? Like... smarter or healthier or something?" She winced, realizing how awkward the question sounded. "I mean, David is all about the DNA thing, maybe it's like that?"

Riley burst out laughing, doubling over and clutching her stomach. "Oh my god, Reagan! Where do you even come up with this stuff?" She had to pause to catch her breath. "Smarter sperm? Seriously? No, Reagan, Junior's cream pies do not magically turn us into geniuses or make us younger."

Emma, ever the sweet and gentle soul, looked a little flustered but managed a smile. "Riley's right. Junior's cum is delicious, but it doesn't grant superpowers. David's wives are smart because they work hard, they take care of themselves, they take care of each other, and they're encouraged to keep learning." Riley nodded in agreement. "Exactly! David's smart enough to surround himself with capable women and give them the space to grow. It's about empowerment, not enchanted ejaculate."

Emma added with a sigh, "Most modern women want to escape reality and are just trying to make it without men stepping on them, we are grateful to have a place where we can be ourselves." Callie, who was also suppressing a chuckle, added. "Besides," she added with a smirk, "I'm pretty sure Reagan's theory would require a whole lot of...scientific experimentation. And honestly, who's got the time for that?"

Reagan blushed, but her curiosity wasn't entirely quenched. "Okay, okay, I get it. It's a silly theory. But Darrel is convinced. He thinks it's why his wives always want to have sex with him." Riley threw her hands up in mock exasperation. "Darrel, bless his heart, is a walking encyclopedia of conspiracy theories. I wouldn't trust him to tell you what day it is!" She paused. "Look, I'm not saying David's not a...satisfying partner. He probably makes those women feel sexy, desired. It's confidence, Reagan, not chromosomes!"

"And let's be real," Riley continued, fanning herself with the map. "If you had eight other women all vying for… his attention, would you really want to be the one who's not interested in his affections?" Emma giggled, covering her mouth with her hand. Callie choked back a laugh, and even Reagan couldn't help but crack a smile. "Okay, okay, point taken," Reagan conceded, still looking thoughtful.

Riley adopted a serious expression, puffing out her chest slightly. "Okay, listen up, ladies. Forget chromosomes. Forget pheromones. Let me lay some truth on you." She paused dramatically, looking around as if checking for eavesdroppers. "David knew this was all going to happen." Emma gasped. "Knew? You mean the… the EMP?" "Yep!" Riley nodded emphatically. "David spent his life preparing for it, ever since he was a kid, and he wasn't going to let anyone stop him."

Callie raised an eyebrow. "So, you're saying he predicted the apocalypse and built this whole place knowing it would happen?" "Not exactly!" Riley's voice dropped to a conspiratorial whisper. "He experienced it. This exact one. For seven years, alone!" Reagan looked bewildered. "But what does that have to do with… wanting to be with him?"

Riley smirked. "It's about more than just wanting, honey. It's about fulfilling a primal need. His wives saw his confidence, his strength, his desire to take care of those he loved, and they wanted to be as close to that as possible." She spread her arms wide, gesturing towards the horizon. "This ranch, this community, wouldn't exist without him. We wouldn't exist!"

"And the more time they spent with him," Riley continued, her voice laced with genuine admiration, "the more they witnessed his brilliance and the extent of his foresight. Even before the EMP, they believed in him. Once the lights went out, I imagine their faith in him hit critical mass." Riley clapped her hands together, startling a nearby lizard. "Now, some might say they worship him." She paused, a gleam in her eye. "And they do. Not as a god, mind you, but as a person deserving their complete and absolute submission."

Several hours later, Riley capped the can of orange marker paint. Sweat beading on her forehead despite the slight breeze. "Alright, ladies, Phase One complete. We've officially defaced the hillside with Aidan's grand vision." Callie adjusted the brim of her cap and consulted her notepad. "Are we sure this is the best spot? The ground slopes pretty steeply here. Excavation's gonna be a bitch."

Reagan, lounging against a sun-baked boulder, fanned herself with a page from her own notebook. "Yeah, and it's hot as hell. I'm pretty sure I saw a tumbleweed die of dehydration." Emma piped up. "Aidan said he wants to build into the hillside, not on top of it. Something about structural integrity and... thermal regulation?" She wrinkled her nose, clearly not an engineer.

Riley chuckled. "Exactly! He wants a hobbit hole for blacksmithing. Think of it, cool and dark, fire-resistant...

perfect for hammering hot metal. Plus, it'll be half-buried, practically invisible from a distance. Makes us look less like a juicy target." She grinned mischievously. "And the best part? No back-breaking digging for us! Aidan's planning on using dynamite."

Reagan jolted upright. "Dynamite?! Seriously?" Her eyes widened. "I thought we were going for 'subtle' and 'low profile,' not attracting every rattlesnake and displaced survivalist within a fifty-mile radius!" Riley waved a dismissive hand. "Relax, drama queen. He's not blowing up the whole damn hill. Just enough to loosen the dirt and rock. Timed just right, it'll break it all up nice and easy."

Reagan visibly deflated, relief washing over her face. "Oh, thank God. For a second I thought we were going to have to dig the whole thing out by hand. That would have been absolutely brutal." Callie tapped her pen against her notepad. "Dynamite could still cause problems. Part of the hillside might collapse, you know? We need to factor that into the design." She squinted, tracing an imaginary line with her finger along the slope. "On the plus side, at least we know which direction the water will flow after the blast. Natural drainage is a big win."

The girls huddled together, their conversation shifting to the more technical aspects of the project. Riley, despite her initial flippancy, was actually quite organized. She pulled out a detailed schematic, pointing out the planned dimensions and explaining Aidan's proposed support structures.

Emma, ever eager to please, took notes diligently, asking questions about the ventilation system and the placement of the forge. Reagan, still a bit skeptical, voiced her concerns about the noise attracting unwanted attention, but Riley assured her that Aidan had a plan for sound dampening.

Just then, a welcome shadow fell over them. Aidan, looking more like a manager than a mechanic, emerged with a tray laden with frosty glasses and a bowl overflowing with trail mix. "How's the future real estate looking, ladies?" he asked, his smile genuine. "Figured you could use a little somethin' to cool down."

The lemonade was tart and sweet, the trail mix a satisfying mix of salty and crunchy. Reagan practically inhaled her glass. "This is amazing, Aidan, thanks. We're still hashing out the details. Callie's worried about the dynamite causing a landslide." Aidan chuckled, running a hand through his perpetually messy hair. "Yeah, it's a valid concern. That's why we're not going full Wile E. Coyote on it. Mark's got some experience from his road construction days. He knows how to handle explosives... mostly." He winked. "Plus, we'll reinforce the back wall like crazy. It needs to be bomber proof anyways." Emma's brow furrowed. "The back wall? What's that for?"

Aidan pointed to where the hillside met the theoretical back of the smithy. "That's what's going to keep the whole damn hill from becoming part of our new forge. Solid bedrock and reinforced concrete. Think of it as a really, really tough retaining wall." Reagan crinkled her nose. "So, dynamite, solid bedrock, retaining walls, drainage... what about all the dirt we dig out? We can't just leave a giant pile of loose soil sitting around."

Aidan grinned. "That's the sneaky part. All the backfill is going to be used to sculpt the area around the smithy. Make it look like it's always been there. Camouflage it, even. We want it to be as invisible as possible from the hilltops. Think hobbit hole, but with more ironwork." "And the noise? Even with soundproofing, hammering metal is going to create a racket." Riley added.

Aidan nodded, impressed by her foresight. "The entire hillside, along with the excavated material we'll pack against the bunker on this side. Like a big earthen sound barrier. It won't be completely silent, of course, but it'll dampen the noise significantly. Plus a earthen structure has some very cool benefits in the winter and summer. We'll have a nice cool work space year round."

A brief, comfortable silence fell over the group as they contemplated the sheer scale of the project. Callie shifted her weight from one foot to the other, then took a breath, deciding this was as good a time as any to ask. "Aidan... can I ask you something?" she began, her tone tentative. "It's a little personal, I guess."

Aidan looked up from the plans, his expression open and curious. "Shoot." "It's about Junior," she said, glancing at Emma, who offered a small, encouraging smile. "I've noticed you and Brian have these... well, specialized skills. You're the engineer and mechanic. Brian's the tech wizard and gardener. But Junior... he's all combat and stuff. Why doesn't he have a high-tech skill like you guys?"

Aidan chuckled, folding his arms. "That's a good question, Callie. You think Junior's just running around shooting things all day?" "Well, not just shooting things," Callie amended quickly, "but… yeah, kind of. I mean, he's amazing at it, don't get me wrong. But in this world, shouldn't everyone have something… more technical?"

Emma giggled. "Oh, honey, you have no idea." Reagan chimed in. "I see what you mean, Callie. It's like… we need builders and fixers more than soldiers now, right?" Aidan nodded slowly. "You're not wrong, Reagan. But you're underestimating Junior. He's not just a good shot. Think about it, who went to Goodfellow? Who brought back fourteen people who now contribute immensely to our community?"

Riley snorted. "Yeah, but that was 'cause he's a badass. He just ripped that Davis guy apart! That's not exactly a technical skill, is it?" Aidan grinned. "Alright, alright. Fair point. But it's not all about brute force. He's also fluent in several languages. Think about what it takes to learn Japanese, Chinese, Korean and Thai. That's a difficult mastery." "He knows all those languages? Seriously?" Callie asked, her eyes widening.

Aidan nodded. "Seriously, and that's just the ones he learned on top of the two we all knew. The point is, he picked them up to better understand the cultures behind the martial arts he was studying. It's always about knowing people, including our enemies." Emma added, her voice laced with affection, "He's also incredibly skilled with his hands, just… not with circuit boards. Apparently, he can build anything, just like his brothers and sisters."

Aidan continued, "Think about it this way, Callie. Brian's a great gardener, but that's only half the story. He's a momma's boy who gets his kicks from gaming. So yes, Brian knows his way around tech, but his true passion lies elsewhere. Junior chose to focus his skills on people. He's a damn good judge of character, a natural leader, and he has an uncanny ability to connect with people from all walks of life."

Reagan raised an eyebrow. "So, you're saying he's the... people person of the apocalypse?" Aidan threw his head back and laughed. "You could say that! Look, every one of us has a unique path. I gravitated towards engineering because I love making and fixing things. Brian likes his gadgets. Lily's all about feelings. Seth and grace are sneaky as fuck. Junior... he's all about understanding and leading people. And in this new world, that's a pretty damn valuable skill."

He clapped Callie on the shoulder. "Don't underestimate Junior, kid. He's more than just a soldier. He's the reason we were able to gather a group like this in the first place. Building a new world isn't just about erecting structures or coding algorithms, it's about building something with people, and Junior is the best man we have for that job." Callie looked thoughtful, chewing on her lip. "Okay, I get it. So it's not that he can't do the tech stuff, it's that he's chosen to do something different."

Emma, gripping her collar, piped up. "Junior says it's about leverage. He learns enough about everything so he can delegate and problem-solve. He can't be everywhere at once,

69

but he can use his skills to make sure everyone else is in the right place, doing the right thing."

Aidan nodded approvingly. "Leverage, that's the perfect word for it! Dad calls it cultivation." He paused, a wry smile tugging at his lips. "Dad isn't the strongest guy here. Hell, he's not even the smartest. But Dad had the foresight to prepare for all this. He's a strategist, a cultivator." Reagan frowned. "Cultivator? Like... a farmer?"

"Sort of," Aidan chuckled. "Kinda like... a resource manager. He cultivates resources and people. He figures out our strengths, our weaknesses, and then puts us where we can be most effective. That's why he's the Patriarch. He has the big picture in mind." "And you think Junior is like that too?" Callie asked, glancing towards the main house.

"Absolutely," Aidan affirmed. There was a flicker of something akin to pride in his eyes. "If anyone is going to be leading the family in the future, it's going to be Junior. Because he also has leverage. While I can fix a generator, and Brian can code a security system, Junior can get people to want to fix the generator and code the security system. He inspires loyalty, he encourages cooperation, and he makes sure everyone feels like they're contributing. That's a leader, and that's exactly what we need."

He paused, noticing Callie's continued fascination. "Why the sudden interest in Junior's skillset, Callie? Planning on enlisting his services?" Callie blushed, caught off guard. "No, it's just... I see how Emma, Riley, and Olivia are with him. They seem so... content. I guess I'm just curious."

Emma, who had been quietly marking in her notebook, looked up, a soft smile gracing her lips. "Before Junior rescued me, I... I didn't know what it was like to feel safe, to feel cherished. He's so capable, so strong... but he's also incredibly kind. I didn't know about all of his skills until after I married him, but knowing my husband is so capable, and that I get to be his wife," she took a long breath, "feels like a power fantasy come true."

Riley snorted. "That's not all, Callie. Junior isn't all tactics and skill." She trailed off, a distant, almost dreamy look in her eyes. "The sex is phenomenal." She shuddered subtly, a blush creeping up her neck. "The intensity of the orgasms... it's unlike anything I've ever experienced." Reagan, who had been poking at the ground with her boot, suddenly straightened up. "Woah, woah, ladies, let's keep it to a low simmer, alright? We got work to do."

Callie, however, was riveted. The casual way they talked about relationships, the almost reverent tone they used when talking about Junior, it was all so... foreign. "So," she began hesitantly, "would it be... inappropriate... to ask Junior to show me the... pleasures he offers?"

The question hung in the hot air. Emma's eyes widened slightly, and Riley's mouth dropped open. Reagan choked on a laugh, clapping Callie on the shoulder. "Girl, you don't waste any time, do you?" Reagan said, still chuckling. "Look, Junior is... generous. But he's also married. Are you sure you want to step into that particular minefield?"

Callie frowned. "But... wasn't it Junior who rescued us from Goodfellow? Weren't you all in the same position as

71

me? Weren't you all suffering?" She gestured between them. "You were all refugees, just like me. What makes your suffering so special that it earned you a place at his side, and mine... doesn't?"

Callie pressed her advantage, her voice gaining confidence. "So, because you were there, because you were suffering, that you got... chosen? I was there. I was suffering! I just... I didn't know how to act! I wasn't coy enough, or brave enough, to jump in his arms immediately. Should I be penalized for that? Is that really fair?"

Riley snorted, earning a glare from Emma. "Coy? Honey, 'coy' ain't exactly the word I'd use to describe how we got Junior's attention. More like... transparent honesty." Reagan sighed, the amusement fading from her face, replaced by a thoughtful frown. "Look, Callie, it's not about fair or unfair. Honestly, life ain't fair, especially not after the world went to hell in a handbasket."

Callie crossed her arms, her lower lip jutting out. "I don't give a shit about fair anymore! I mean, look around! David has nine wives! Nine! And Junior has three. How is that fair?" She threw her arms up in exasperation. "It's a picture of unfairness, etched in the goddamn Texas sky!" "It's different, Callie," Emma said softly, her voice laced with a sincerity that cut through the simmering tension. "David provides. Having multiple wives allows David to do that more effectively. It's a... a system."

Callie rolled her eyes. "A system that leaves me out! I don't want to get stuck marrying Mike!" She shuddered dramatically. "Or waiting eighteen years for Lucas or Tyler to grow up! Seriously, what are my options?" She looked at each of them pleadingly. "David has a hierarchy to his wives, right? Jessica's his favorite, Tiffany's the matriarch... Couldn't Junior do the same? Couldn't he have... I don't know... a 'beta' wife program? I just want to be included!"

Riley's laughter echoed slightly, a hand clamped over her mouth. "A 'beta wife' program? You're killing me, Callie! You should pitch that idea to David. I bet he'd be intrigued." Her eyes twinkled mischievously. Callie, ignoring Riley's amusement, stomped her foot lightly on the dirt. "It's not funny, Riley! I'm serious! What are my options? Seriously. What? I don't want to be the last single person at the ranch when I'm, like, forty!"

Reagan tapped her chin. "Well, there's Noah. He's single. Callie immediately scrunched her nose, a dramatic shudder running through her frame. "Noah? Oh, please. He's not my type, and more importantly, I'm definitely not his type. Have you seen his type? He likes... he likes meaty Mexican chicks with big boobs. Quiet, intense types. Not... not bubbly blondes who talk too much." She gestured emphatically to herself. "I'm like the human equivalent of a sparkling soda. Noah's more of a dark roast coffee guy."

Emma offered a small smile. "Noah's a good man, Callie, but you're right, he does seem to prefer a certain... quiet strength." Callie threw her hands up again. "Exactly! And it's not fair! Look at David. He's got variety! Five blondes, two Asians, two brunettes. Big boobs, small boobs and everything in between. He's got the whole buffet! And Junior? My man Junior, who I totally respect and admire, by the way," she added hastily, as if Junior might be listening in the twilight, "he's got Olivia and Emma, both gorgeous brunettes, and Riley, our fiery redhead. Not a single blonde in the bunch! None! It's a blonde wasteland over there!"

Riley snorted, pushing a stray hair off her face. "So, you're saying Junior needs to diversify his portfolio, and you're the blue-chip stock he's missing?" Callie's eyes lit up, ignoring the sarcasm. "Precisely! I'm unique! I'm bubbly, I'm... I'm vivacious! I'm a good worker! I can cook! I'm not afraid of the dark, mostly! I just... I want to be part of something. I want to contribute, like Emma said. Like David's system! A beta wife could totally contribute!" She knew, even as the words tumbled out, how ridiculous she sounded. She was grasping at straws, flailing wildly in the sea of her own unfulfilled romantic aspirations. But damn it, she was going to make her case.

She turned to Riley, her pleading gaze intensified in the dim light. "Riley, you're close to him, right? You can talk to him. You can put in a good word for me. Just tell him I'm... I'm highly adaptable. And very, very honest." She leaned in conspiratorially. "And if he thinks it's a 'beta wife' program, that's fine. I'll take it. It's better than waiting for Lucas's balls to drop, right?"

Riley sighed, rubbing her temples. The heat was getting to everyone, she figured. "Callie, I get it. You're lonely, you wanna secure your place. But Junior's not some company you can apply to. He's...Junior. And his whole 'one alpha, three submissives' thing is already pushing the limits of sanity. Especially in that shoebox we call an apartment."

Emma piped up softly. "She's right, Callie. It's...crowded. We barely have room to breathe, let alone swing a cat." "I'm not a cat!" Callie protested, throwing her hands up. "And I don't need space! I'm small! I can curl up in a corner, I can... I can learn to sleep standing up!" Riley burst out laughing. "Okay, now you're just being absurd. Look, I'll talk to him, alright? But I'm not promising anything. Junior makes his own decisions, mostly. Especially when it comes to...wives."

Callie, her face brightening slightly, grabbed Riley's hand. "Thank you, Riley! You're the best! I owe you big time." She paused, then leaned close to Aidan. "Hey, Aidan, is it true the apartments are seriously small? Like, claustrophobia-inducing small?" Aidan chuckled, a warm, genuine sound. "Claustrophobic? No. Cozy? Definitely. Let's just say David wasn't exactly expecting large families, or another harem breaking out, when he designed the Apartment bunker. It was more of an afterthought, really. A place to put people who needed a place to be."

Callie's face fell a little. "So, it's hopeless then? No chance of fitting in without someone getting squished from lack of space?" Aidan considered her for a moment, a thoughtful expression on his face. "Not necessarily. Look, I helped design this place. I know the blueprints inside and out. It's... configurable." Callie perked up instantly. "Configurable? What does that mean?"

Aidan gestured towards the work shed. "The apartments are designed to be modular. They're all pretty much the same size, but the walls aren't load-bearing. You could... technically, combine them or reconfigure them. Make a larger one." He paused, a glint in his eye. "Even the guest rooms in the garage bunker. But there's a catch." Callie's enthusiasm waned slightly. "A catch? There's always a catch."

"Yeah," Aidan confirmed. "You can only combine them if they're empty. We're not exactly going to evict anyone to make room for Junior's fifth...or fourth...wife. I lose count." He grinned wryly. Callie's eyes widened. An idea was clearly forming. "So, if, and I mean if someone were, hypothetically speaking, to...convince Junior to let me move in..."

Aidan raised an eyebrow. "Hypothetically speaking, if that were to happen, and Riley, Emma, and Olivia were okay with sharing a combined apartment... then it might be possible to reconfigure some of the walls after, if no one complains about it." He winked. "Emphasis on the might." Callie threw her arms around Aidan in a hug, nearly knocking his tablet out of his hand. "Aidan, you're amazing! Thank you!"

Chapter 17:

Grace's Strategic Siege

"Alright, Michelangelo, ease up on the throttle a bit!" Darrel yelled, as he meticulously separated stones and rocks with Brian, Andrew, Noah, Reagan, and Callie. The scene resembled a bizarre archaeological dig, only instead of unearthing ancient artifacts, they were prepping for Aidan's grand smithy scheme. "Easy for you to say, you get to play in the dirt!" Caleb retorted, his voice strained. The backhoe sputtered and lurched, nearly embedding its bucket into the hillside. "This thing handles like a shopping cart full of greased watermelons!"

While Caleb battled the rebellious backhoe, another team was out scavenging. David, ever the patriarch, had dispatched Seth, Eric, Parker, Kyle, Mark, and Junior to gather resources from surrounding towns. They rolled out in a convoy: David's Sedan leading the way, followed by Eric and Parker in the behemoth, and Seth and Kyle bringing up the rear in Elena's armored coupe.

Inside the Sedan, David calmly navigated the pothole-ridden roads. He knew that every trip outside the ranch's fortified perimeter carried risks, but the rewards were essential. "Remember," he said, his voice calm and steady from the radio, "prioritize concrete mix, rebar, and any usable steel."

Kyle kept his eyes glued to the road, his knuckles white on the steering wheel. He was used to high-stress situations, clearing buildings, facing down scavengers, re-chambering a rifle under duress. This, however, was a different kind of danger zone. Seth had been quiet for the last twenty miles, his observant eyes taking in the desolate landscape and, more often than not, flickering over to study Kyle's profile.

"So," Seth finally said, his voice calm and even. "We need to talk." Kyle braced himself. "About what? The rebar situation? 'Cause if Parker thinks we can substitute galvanized pipe, he's got another thing comin'." "No," Seth replied, turning in his seat. He had their mother's sweet face but David's unnerving directness. "About Grace." Kyle's grip on the wheel tightened. "What about her?" he asked, his tone a little too casual. "She's fine. Helped me sort brass casings this morning."

Seth didn't smile. "I know. She told me. She also told me a lot of other things." He paused, letting the statement hang in the air. "Kyle... are you really having sex with my sister?" The coupe swerved slightly as Kyle's foot twitched on the accelerator. He coughed, a dry, panicked sound. "Whoa, kid. Where's this coming from? That's... that's a hell of an accusation."

"It's not an accusation, it's a question," Seth said, completely unfazed. "Grace has been different since your 'date night.' She refers to your apartment as 'our place', and don't think I haven't noticed her change in behavior. Grace is happy. Like, annoyingly happy. So, are you?" "She's a great kid," Kyle finally managed, his voice a strained croak. "A big

78

help. Reminds me of... well, she's got a good head on her shoulders."

Seth just watched him, his expression placid. It was unnervingly like being interrogated by a much smaller, gentler version of David. "A 'good head doesn't explain why she's taken to darning your socks. I didn't even know she knew how to darn socks." Kyle's jaw worked silently. He had wondered where that neatly repaired sock had come from. "She's... considerate."

"She's a predator," Seth corrected him, though his tone was conversational, as if they were discussing the migratory patterns of birds. "She's been hunting you for years, Kyle. We all saw it. It was like watching a nature documentary. I think Jennifer and Jessica actually had a running bet on when she'd finally make her move." Kyle's face flushed. "A predator? Seth, she's your sister. She's a sweet girl."

"She is a sweet girl," Seth agreed easily. "A sweet girl who spent the last three years meticulously planning your capture. It was a long, strategic campaign. I have to admire the dedication." Every word was a precisely aimed dart, and Kyle felt himself deflating in the driver's seat. He couldn't even argue; he remembered everything she had done, but had naively written them off as a teenager's passing interests.

Seth leaned back in his seat, folding his arms. "There's also the... biological evidence." "The what?" Kyle asked, dread coiling in his stomach. "Well," Seth began, his tone now bordering on clinical. "For the last couple of years, she's been... relieving her own sexual tension, if you catch my meaning. We were either sharing a wall or a room together, especially after Lucas and Poppy were born. We respected each other's privacy, of course, but nothing gets past me, Kyle. Nothing." He paused, letting the implication hang in the air. Kyle felt like he was going to be sick.

"About three weeks ago," Seth continued calmly, "it just... stopped. Completely. Cold turkey. I figured it was either she lost interest, or she was finally getting the real deal. Considering she now spends eighty percent of her free time in your apartment and comes back smelling like your soap, I'm leaning toward the latter."

He could feel Seth's calm, observant gaze on him from the passenger seat. There was no gloating in it, which was somehow worse. It was just... factual. Like a mechanic diagnosing a faulty engine. 'Well, here's your problem, sir. Your girlfriend has been meticulously plotting your romantic downfall for years, and the primary evidence is a sudden cessation of her masturbatory habits. That'll be fifty bucks.'

Kyle swallowed, his throat dry. He couldn't refute the evidence. He couldn't deny the logic. He could only do what any cornered, thirty-two year-old man does when being intellectually dismantled by a teenager: lash out with a clumsy, desperate deflection. "Oh yeah?" Kyle grunted, his voice tight. He forced a smirk, hoping it looked less like a grimace of pain. "You've got it all figured out, huh, kid? What about you, then?" He jerked his head toward Seth. "You and Bonnie. Are you two... 'getting the real deal' yet? Or is she still in the planning stages of her campaign?"

He let out a slow, deliberate sigh, the kind a weary parent gives a child who has just asked a spectacularly foolish question. "You know, Kyle," he began, his voice dropping into a tone of quiet, almost pitying reason. "For a guy who just got comprehensively outmaneuvered by my sister, you're surprisingly eager to wander into another minefield."

Seth shifted in his seat, the leather creaking softly. "But since you asked, and we're apparently going to be brothers-in-law or whatever convoluted title our family structure dictates, I'll be direct." He met Kyle's gaze, his own clear and steady. "No. We have not had sex. And we won't be having sex for a very long time." Kyle felt a brief, idiotic flash of victory, which was immediately extinguished by Seth's follow-up.

"However," Seth continued, raising a single finger as if lecturing a class, "to answer the spirit of your rather crass question, yes, we are making progress. Good progress, actually. We haven't advanced beyond some fairly enthusiastic kissing, but I have to admit, Bonnie has... well, she has an intuitive grasp of intimacy that I admit I wasn't expecting."

He paused, a flicker of something that might have been a wry smile touching his lips. "I attribute it to environmental osmosis. Growing up in a house with our father and his nine wives, not to mention all the other happy couples... she's been surrounded by a sheer volume of sexually confident and affectionate women for over a year. She sees intimacy as a natural, positive expression, not some taboo secret. It means she's not awkward or shy about it. She's... earnest. It's refreshing."

Kyle could only stare, his mouth slightly open. He had tried to put Seth on the back foot and instead had received a clinical, yet strangely sweet, analysis of his twelve-year-old girlfriend's kissing prowess. "Is it difficult to resist the urge to... escalate the situation?" Seth's expression turned serious, the brief levity gone. "More than I anticipated, if I'm being honest.

She's a wonderful girl, and she's going to be a phenomenal woman. The temptation is there." He looked out the window again, at the silhouette of the massive truck ahead of them. "But we both know that indulging in that would be profoundly irresponsible. She's twelve, Kyle. The experience would be more about transgression than enjoyment, and that's not what I want for her. Or for us. Building something real takes patience. It's a foundation, not a race."

The unspoken comparison hung between them, thick and heavy. Seth, at fifteen, was exercising a level of restraint and foresight with a twelve-year-old that Kyle, at thirty-two, had failed to muster with Seth's own twin sister. Kyle felt his face heat up, a fresh wave of shame washing over him that had nothing to do with being caught and everything to do with being so thoroughly, and gently, shown up.

Kyle stared at the lights of the truck in front of him, his knuckles white on the steering wheel. He felt fifteen again, but not in a good way. He felt like the clumsy, hormone-addled teenager he once was, sitting next to a man who, despite being half his age, possessed the wisdom of a seasoned philosopher. To be lectured on romantic restraint by his fifteen-year-old hookup's twin brother was a circle of hell he hadn't known existed. The shame was a physical thing, a hot stone in his gut.

He cleared his throat, the sound rough and loud in the enclosed space. "I... uh..." He trailed off, unable to formulate a defense because there wasn't one. He exhaled a sharp, frustrated breath. "You're a better man than I am, Seth. That's all there is to it." Seth turned from the window, his expression unreadable in the dim dashboard light. He didn't gloat or agree. Instead, a small, knowing smile touched the corners of his mouth. "It's not about being a 'better man,' Kyle. It's about facing a different opponent." He shifted in his seat, turning slightly to face him. "Bonnie is... methodical. She's sweet and she plans things out, but she's still a kid. There's a boundary there that's bright and clear."

He paused before continuing. "My sister," he said, and the smile became a little more wry, "Grace is not methodical. Grace is a hurricane. When she decides she wants something, she's like a heat-seeking missile with a really good sense of fashion. You weren't dealing with a campaign of subtle hints; you were withstanding a siege." Kyle blinked, looking over at the teenager. A siege. That was... surprisingly accurate.

"Honestly," Seth continued, his voice dropping, "the rest of us were taking bets. Junior thought you'd crack last Christmas. I had my money on her birthday in March. You holding the line for as long as you did... it's actually impressive. You kept her off you for, what, a few years of concerted effort? That's not a failure, Kyle. That's a valiant last stand. Don't look so shell-shocked," Seth said, his voice imbued with a calm logic that was unnervingly similar to his father's. "You're thinking of it as a series of random events. It wasn't. It was a campaign, Kyle. And every single move was calculated."

Kyle finally turned from the window, his expression a mixture of disbelief and dawning horror. "Calculated? Seth, she's a kid. She…"

"She's my sister," Seth interrupted, his tone matter-of-fact. "And she's David's daughter. You think she doesn't know how to play the long game? A low groan escaped Kyle's lips as he slumped further into the luxurious leather seat. He felt less like a man and more like a chess piece, moved across the board by a grandmaster he didn't even know was playing. "Why?" he finally asked, his voice rough. "Why go to all that trouble?"

Seth adjusted his position, the analytical light in his eyes softening slightly. "At first? It was practical." He said the word clinically, as if discussing livestock breeding. "You're strong, you're skilled, you're loyal to the family, and your sister's relationship to my father is a bonus. In a world like this, you're a… suitable reproductive partner."

Kyle flinched as if he'd been slapped. "A what?" "A high-value asset for ensuring the continuation and strength of the family line," Seth clarified, completely deadpan. "She saw potential." The sheer audacity of it, the cold biological assessment, left Kyle speechless. He was just… breeding stock? But before the indignation could fully set in, Seth continued, his voice changing, losing its clinical edge and gaining a hint of warmth.

"But then something changed. It stopped being a project." Seth looked out his own window for a moment. "It was how you reacted. Every time she pushed a little too far, you pushed back. You didn't just ignore her; you'd scold her. You'd remind her of the optics, of what was appropriate. You never took advantage, not once. You treated her with a frustrating, infuriating amount of respect."

Seth looked back at him, and for the first time, Kyle saw the genuine kid behind the hyper-intelligent facade. "She wasn't used to that. She's used to people being intimidated by her or coddling her. You were the first man besides Dad or Junior who treated her like a real woman, a person who needed guidance, not just an objective to be won. Your resistance, the very thing that drove you crazy, is what made her fall in love with you."

The word hung in the air between them, heavier than any weapon in the car. Love. Not a siege. Not a campaign. Not a biological imperative. Kyle checked the rearview mirror out of pure reflex, his gaze catching the determined line of his own jaw. He saw not a failure, but a man who had held a line out of principle, only to find that the line itself had become the prize. "So the whole 'heat-seeking missile' thing…" Kyle started, trailing off. "Was armed with more than just teenage hormones," Seth finished with a wry smile. "It was armed with a strategy guide. Honestly, Kyle, you never stood a chance."

"Alright, fine," Kyle finally conceded. "We... we are. Having sex." He felt a flush of heat creep up his neck. "But she... she always initiates it. Every single time. I'm just... responding." Seth nodded sagely, as if Kyle had just confirmed a complex physics equation. "I know."

This threw Kyle for another loop. "Then explain this to me, you brilliant little bastard," he grumbled, a hint of his usual exasperation returning. "She's militant about using condoms. Every. Single. Time. And those things run out. If this was all some grand strategy to secure a superior breeding partner, wouldn't that be... you know... completely counterproductive?"

Seth sighed, a long-suffering sound that belonged to a man three times his age. He looked at Kyle with an expression that was one part pity, two parts amusement. "Kyle, for a guy with your skill, you are completely dense when it comes to this. It stopped being a strategy. That's the entire point. That night, on Date Night? That was the final move of the campaign. Everything since then has been... the victory lap."

Kyle just stared at him, utterly baffled. "She's not trying to have your baby right now," Seth explained slowly, as if to a child. "She's trying to have you. The person. The intimacy. The closeness. She's a girl who is deeply in love and wants to sleep with her man without the immediate consequence of getting pregnant in the middle of an apocalypse. It's not strategy. It's just... wanting you."

The simplicity of it was staggering. All his theories, his fears of being a target, a genetic specimen, they all evaporated in the face of that simple, terrifying truth. She loved him. A different kind of anxiety began to settle in Kyle's gut. As if reading his mind, Seth's playful expression faded, replaced by a flicker of genuine concern. He turned his gaze back to the road ahead. "Honestly, that's what actually worries me now."

"What does?" Kyle asked, his voice quiet.

"Her focus," Seth said, his tone dropping. "Grace's greatest asset, besides her intelligence, has always been her singular, almost ruthless focus on a goal. But now... her goal is achieved. It's you. And love... love distracts. What happens when we're clearing a building and she's more worried about where you are than where the threats are? What happens if she hesitates because she's thinking about keeping you safe instead of herself?"

Hours later, the rumble of the Behemoth, was a sound of triumphant return, its V8 engine a guttural bass note against the chirping of night insects. Headlights sliced through the oppressive darkness of the Texas night, illuminating the dust kicked up by the convoy. David's sedan pulled in first, followed by the hulking Behemoth, with Elena's armored coupe bringing up the rear. As doors opened, the night shift crew, already buzzing with energy, swarmed the vehicles.

"Excellent haul, Junior," David commented, his voice calm and steady as he stepped out of the sedan. He gave his son a proud clap on the shoulder before his eyes scanned the massive cutout in the hillside, where several large piles of freshly excavated rock sat waiting. "And it seems Aidan's crew has been just as productive."

Kyle practically fell out of the coupe, his muscles screaming in protest from the long drive and the strain of heaving materials. The conversation with Seth echoed in his skull, each word a phantom weight added to the 80-pound bags of concrete mix he now had to help unload. He watched as Brian and the others formed a human chain, efficiently moving rebar and bags near the hillside. But all Kyle could think about was Seth's parting words. Love distracts.

An hour later, covered in a fine layer of dust and sweat, Kyle trudged toward the apartment bunker. The physical exhaustion was a welcome distraction, but now, in the relative quiet, the anxiety gnawed at him again. He unlocked his apartment, the door swinging open to a world completely alien to the one he'd just left.

The air smelled of seared steak and garlic. Soft light from a lamp cast a warm glow across the small living area. And there, standing at the small kitchenette, was Grace. She was wearing one of his old, worn-out band t-shirts, the fabric hanging loosely off her frame. Her hair was piled messily on her head, and she hummed softly as she stirred something in a pan.

She turned as the door clicked shut, a bright smile instantly lighting up her face. "Hey, you." Her eyes did a quick, observant scan, taking in his disheveled state. "You look like you wrestled The Behemoth and lost." Kyle managed a weary smile. "Something like that. Smells amazing." "I figured you'd be starving," she said, her expression softening with a tenderness that made his stomach clench for reasons entirely unrelated to hunger. Before he could even respond, she wiped her hands on a dishtowel, set down her spatula, and turned off the burner. "Dinner can wait five minutes. Go sit down. I'm running you a bath."

He just stared, utterly dumbfounded, as she breezed past him into the small bathroom. He heard the rush of water filling the tub. Kyle sank onto the edge of the small sofa, the worn cushion groaning under his weight. He rested his elbows on his knees, burying his face in his grimy hands. Seth's voice was a low, concerned murmur in his memory. "What happens when we're clearing a building and she's more worried about where you are than where the threats are?"

The sound of rushing water from the small bathroom was a soothing balm on Kyle's frayed nerves. He hadn't even realized he'd stopped breathing until a long, shuddering sigh escaped his lungs. He felt less like a man and more like a collection of aches held together by grit and road dust.

Grace appeared in the doorway, a small, knowing smile on her lips. The old band t-shirt she wore, one he hadn't seen in years, swam on her, the faded logo of a long-defunct metal group stretched across her chest. "C'mon, big guy," she said, her voice soft but firm, leaving no room for argument. "Bath's ready. Up you get."

He wanted to protest, to say he could wash himself, but the effort felt monumental. Instead, he let her take his hand. Her fingers, though small, were strong as they wrapped around his, and she pulled him to his feet with surprising ease. He stumbled after her like a tired bear being led by a surprisingly determined forest sprite.

The bathroom was filled with steam, the air thick and warm. Grace didn't hesitate. She began unbuttoning his filthy shirt, her movements methodical and efficient, completely devoid of any coyness or theatrics. It was the same practical focus she applied to cleaning a rifle or inventorying supplies. He just stood there, swaying slightly, letting her peel away the layers of his exhausting day. His shirt, his pants, his socks— all were discarded into a neat pile by the door.

"In," she commanded softly, gesturing to the steaming tub. Kyle obeyed, sinking into the hot water with a groan that was equal parts pain and pleasure. The water instantly began to turn a murky grey.

Grace tutted softly. "Right. This shirt's gonna get soaked." Without another word, she pulled the t-shirt over her head, folding it neatly and placing it on the closed toilet lid. She was left in her simple bra and shorts. Then, assessing the potential for splash-back, she unclipped her bra, adding it to the folded shirt. She sat on the wide alcove of the tub, her back against the cool tile, and dipped her feet into the water at the far end. Her bare torso was pale and slender in the humid light, but her posture was all business.

She picked up a washcloth, lathered it with a bar of soap, and began to scrub his back. "You have new knots," she observed, her thumbs digging into the tense muscles of his shoulders. "Was Seth behaving?" "Seth was fine," Kyle mumbled, his head lolling forward. "Kid's a better scout than I ever was. It was the roads… and the scavengers near Dripping Springs."

"Mmm," she hummed, her attention focused on scrubbing the grime from his arms. "Well, you're here now. And you're safe." She said it with such simple, unshakeable conviction that it almost silenced the worried echo of her brother's voice in his head. Almost. Her focus wasn't a distraction; it was an anchor. She didn't worry about him out there; she prepared a sanctuary for him back here.

Once she was satisfied that the initial layer of filth was gone, she leaned over and pulled the plug. The dirty water swirled away with a gurgling sigh. "Alright, first pass complete," she announced, as if it were a military operation.

She rinsed the tub quickly with the handheld shower nozzle before plugging the drain again and turning on the taps. Fresh, clean water began to pour in. Grace reached for a small jar of bath salts, sprinkling a generous amount into the tub, followed by a glug of bubble bath that immediately began to foam. The air, once just smelling of soap, now carried scents of lavender and eucalyptus. "There," she said, her work complete. "Now you can actually relax. I'll have your steak ready when you get out. Medium rare, right?"

She stood, grabbing a small towel to dry her feet with the same practical efficiency she'd displayed all evening. Then, she picked up the folded t-shirt and slipped it back over her head, the familiar worn cotton settling back into place. The moment of vulnerability was over, replaced once again by the comforting, slightly absurd image of this fifteen-year-old girl playing the part of a seasoned, caring wife.

"Don't be long," she said with a final, warm smile before disappearing back into the main room, leaving Kyle soaking in a mountain of bubbles, the smell of sizzling steak now tantalizing his senses. He sank deeper into the water, a weary, incredulous smile touching his lips. Seth had it all wrong. Grace wasn't a liability; she was the whole damn reason he could face the world outside their walls.

After a few more minutes of blissful quiet, he stood, water sluicing off his tired muscles. He dried himself off and found the clothes Grace had left for him on the counter: a pair of soft, grey pajama pants and a faded black t-shirt. Dressed and feeling more human than he had in days, he walked out of the bathroom.

The table was set for two. A thick, perfectly seared steak sat next to a scoop of mashed potatoes with a puddle of melted butter in the center and a pile of green beans. It looked like a picture from a restaurant menu. Grace was already seated, watching him with a contented look on her face. As he pulled out his chair, she rose fluidly, grabbing a pitcher from the small counter. She filled his glass with cool water, the ice clinking softly. As she set the heavy glass down, she leaned her body against his shoulder, then pressed a soft, lingering kiss to his cheek. "Eat up," she murmured.

Kyle picked up his fork, a small, weary smile playing on his lips. "Thanks, Gracie." He cut into the steak. It was a perfect medium-rare, bleeding just the right amount of juice onto the plate. The first bite was sublime. "This is... wow." Grace sat back down, propping her chin on her hand as she watched him eat. "How was the run? Did Seth behave himself?"

"The run was fine," he began, dabbing his mouth with a napkin. "Productive. We got a hell of a lot of rebar and nearly cleaned out a hardware store of their concrete mix. Aidan was thrilled." He paused, taking a long drink of water. Grace waited patiently, her gaze never leaving his face, her expression one of serene interest. She could read him better than anyone, and she knew there was more.

Kyle set his glass down and let out a weary sigh, a faint smile touching his lips. "And to answer your other question... no, Seth did not exactly behave himself." A delicate eyebrow arched on Grace's forehead. "Oh?" "He's fifteen," Kyle said, shaking his head with a mix of frustration and fondness. "And he's your twin. Which apparently gives him an unlimited license to be a pain in my ass." He leaned back in his chair, gesturing with his fork.

Kyle recapped the conversation; the observations, the strategic predatory behavior, Seth's relationship with Bonnie, the bets made between other members of the family, even Grace's masturbation habits. Finally, he shared Seth's concerns. He finished, the words hanging in the air between them. He expected... something. A flash of anger at Seth for his intrusion, a hint of embarrassment for being so thoroughly exposed. But Grace offered none of it. She simply absorbed the information with the placid calm of a deep lake.

After a long moment, she shifted, her expression softening. Her voice, when she spoke, was gentle and devoid of any recrimination. "Kyle," she began, "forget about Seth for a minute. Forget the bets and the gossip." She tilted her head. "When you came home tonight, tired and covered in dust, did you enjoy the hot bath I drew for you? Did you enjoy this meal?"

The question was so simple, so direct, that it completely disarmed him. The tension in his shoulders eased. He looked from his half-eaten steak to her earnest face, and a genuine, warm smile finally broke through his weariness. "Yeah, Gracie," he admitted, his voice softening. "I did. More than you know. It felt... incredibly welcoming. Intimate."

A satisfied, smile touched Grace's lips. It was the smile of a job well done, of a plan perfectly executed. "It's supposed to," she said, her tone matter-of-fact, as if stating the most obvious truth in the world. "I am your wife, after all. And that's the only thing that matters."

Chapter 18:

The Foundations of David

The air, thick enough to swim through, was filled with the rhythmic, grumbling churn of the portable concrete mixer and the scent of sweat and wet cement. For Aidan, supervising the construction of the new Smithy felt less like managing a project and more like attempting to wrangle a six-man comedy troupe in the middle of a societal collapse. "My back is screaming in languages I didn't even know it spoke," Mark grunted, heaving another bag of cement mix into the maw of the mixer.

Down in the massive, rectangular pit framed with wooden forms, Kyle and Seth continued to push and agitate the concrete as Marvin dumped wheelbarrow after wheelbarrow of concrete into the rebar reinforced foundation. Kyle, seemed to enjoy this project more than most. Beside him, Seth was a study in earnest concentration, his brow furrowed as he vibrated the mix with a long pole, trying to shake out any potential air bubbles. "Aidan, are we sure this slump is right?" he called up, his voice cracking slightly. "Feels a little stiff."

Before Aidan could answer, Eric, who was positioning a grid of rebar for the next section of wall with Scott, chimed in. "Just keep poking it, kid. It's concrete, not your girlfriend. It'll loosen up." Scott, grunted in agreement, wiping a forearm across his glistening forehead. "If it's too loose, it won't hold.

Same with concrete, same with teenage boys." He shot a pointed look at Seth.

Aidan suppressed a smile. "It's fine, Seth. The mix is designed for low slump to give us higher strength. Just keep working it. You're doing great." Seth, unsatisfied, kept at it. "But…the floor won't be smooth, will it? I mean, with this rough mix…" Kyle snorted, ceasing his shoveling for a moment. "Seth, we're building a smithy, not a skating rink. A few bumps in the floor aren't going to hurt anybody." Marvin nodded enthusiastically. "Exactly. Imperfect texture gives it character! You know, like a well-worn leather belt, or a grizzled old warrior… made of concrete."

Suddenly, a loud clang echoed from the direction of the Behemoth. All heads turned. David, Brian, and Lily were offloading the monstrous, twenty-foot steel I-beams that would form the roof supports, stacking them neatly near the hillside where the smithy would be partially buried.

Scott, wiping his brow again, shook his head. "I'm just glad I'm not the one moving those things." Marvin, eyes wide, watched David and Brian on each end of a bundle of I-beams, carrying them with an almost casual air. "Yeah, why's that, Scott? You think they're heavy?" Scott chuckled. "Heavy? Each one of those I-beams probably weighs close to two hundred pounds! Each! And your talking about that being heavy? Good lord!"

Marvin continued to watch, mouth agape. Lily, meanwhile, was single-handedly hoisting beams down from the truck bed, tossing them to David and Brian with the ease of tossing around firewood. Marvin slowly turned back to the concrete, a dazed look in his eyes. "Suddenly, my back doesn't hurt so bad anymore," he mumbled. "Or, you know, maybe it does, but I just don't want to mention it."

Scott clapped Marvin on the shoulder. "Don't sweat it, kid. Just remember, their strength comes with a price. It's a responsibility they can't escape, that's why they do what they do. The rest of us are just trying to keep up." Marvin's gaze drifted back to David, Lily and Brian as they moved another bundle of steel beams. "Say, Aidan," he said, lowering his voice as he approached. "Between you, Junior, and Brian, who's the strongest?"

Aidan leaned on his shovel, considering the question. "Junior, definitely. He's built like a brick shithouse, but he trained for that. Brian's got size on his side, so he's probably second. I'm… well, I'm the nether." Marvin considered this. "So, you're saying you're closer to a normal man's strength?" Aidan laughed "Not quite, I can still lift an engine block with ease." Aidan pointed at David and Brian. "Those two are about the same. They could do that for an hour before it really burns. I might last 50 minutes before I need a break."

Over in the barn, Josh was giving Bruticus, the larger of the miniature cows, a vigorous brushing. Tiffany supervised with a practiced eye, while Sara watched, her baby Jake gurgling happily in a carrier strapped to her chest. "You gotta get right in there, Josh," Tiffany instructed. "They love that undercoat getting brushed out. Keeps 'em cool in this heat."

Josh, a man who clearly preferred wrangling hogs to pampering miniature cattle, grunted in response. "Yes,

Ma'am." He glanced over at Bruticus, who was now attempting to lick his face. "This little fella sure is friendly. Maybe too friendly." "He thinks you're a salt lick, Honey," Tiffany chuckled, perched on a stool and observing the scene with amusement. "Just try to ignore him. Focus on the brushing."

Sara, meanwhile, had moved on to Rita, a miniature zebu cow with darker hair. The cow seemed far more amenable to the process than Bruticus, standing patiently as Sara worked the shampoo into her coat. Jake was having the time of his life. He squealed with delight, batting at the suds with his tiny hands and feet, creating a bubbly mess. "This is amazing," Sara exclaimed, pausing to wipe a stray bubble from Jake's face. "It's gotta be almost twenty degrees cooler in here than outside. How do you guys manage to keep it so comfortable?"

Tiffany hopped off the stool. "Aidan designed the system," she said. "It's basically a climate-controlled fortress for our livestock. We had to make sure it remained at 65 degrees or lower." Josh wiped his forehead with the back of his hand, leaving a streak of cow slobber. "I use to think David just wanted to spoil the animals, but this isn't about comfort, it's about keeping them alive, isn't it?"

"It's going to get a lot worse, Josh," Tiffany said, her tone turning serious. "The weather patterns are becoming more erratic. Droughts, flash floods, sudden freezes… it's a nightmare. Most livestock just won't survive in the long run." She gestured around the barn, encompassing the comfortable temperature, the reinforced structure, and the meticulous care being given to the miniature cattle. "David anticipated this. He knew we needed to protect our food sources. The miniature breeds don't need as much food or water, but still produce enough milk and meat."

Sara nodded thoughtfully, continuing to massage shampoo into Rita's coat. "So this isn't just about keeping the cows comfy. It's about ensuring our survival." Sara paused, her hands still buried in Rita's surprisingly soft fur. She looked at Tiffany, a dawning horror spreading across her face. "How... how bad is it going to get?" Tiffany sighed, a deep, world-weary sound. "Think triple digits, Sara. We're talking 130 degrees in the summer, easy. And winter? Ten below freezing. Maybe lower. We've already had a taste of it, but it's only going to intensify."

Sara's jaw dropped. "One hundred and thirty degrees? Ten below? How do you know this?" Her voice was a shaky whisper. "Are you psychic or something?" Tiffany chuckled, a dry, humorless sound. "Oh honey, if I was psychic, I'd have played the lottery before the EMP. No, we know because David knows." She emphasized his name, a mixture of reverence and utter exasperation in her tone.

Josh, having finished rinsing his cow, let out a low whistle. "Yeah, I had this conversation with mom the other day. It's hard to wrap your head around it. At first, I thought it sounded like a crazy conspiracy theory. But after seeing some of the things David's predicted come true, I started taking his word as gospel. This whole ranch is proof of it."

Sara shifted her weight, the image of Junior's initial sales pitch at the Air Force base flashing through her mind.

She'd been skeptical, to say the least. A "secure family ranch" sounded like something out of a recruitment brochure, and the promise of safety and stability in a world gone mad seemed too good to be true. Then they arrived. The sheer scale of the ranch, the well-stocked bunkers, the elaborate security measures... it was all insane.

Suddenly, everything clicked. The cows weren't just providing milk and beef. They were vital to maintaining a stable ecosystem on the ranch, providing fertilizer for the hydroponics, contributing to the overall food supply. Each carefully planned detail of their self-sufficient existence had been orchestrated by David.

"So, this," Sara gestured with a soapy sponge towards the cows, "is not just about cute little cows giving us milk and burgers?" Josh chuckled, scrubbing diligently behind Bruticus's surprisingly large ears. "Nope. David's got it all figured out, doesn't he?" Tiffany smiled, a touch of weary pride in her eyes. "Everything on this ranch is calculated. This barn... it's his gift to me. For my love and my loyalty." Sara's voice was hushed, almost reverent. "How long has David known about this? About... all of it?"

Tiffany stilled her scrubbing, then looked at Sara, her expression softening. "Since he was thirteen," she said quietly. "He woke up one day with all this knowledge, this... burden. I didn't learn about his plans until I was twenty. I thought he was just an extremely ambitious, albeit socially awkward, teenager." She shook her head, a small smile playing on her lips. "Imagine being a kid and knowing the world is going to end, and having to prepare for it. That's David's life."

Josh chimed in, "Yeah, he's talked about it before. Says it's like living the same awful movie twice. Except this time, he gets to write the ending. And apparently, that ending involves miniature cows." Tiffany started chuckling then, a sound that bubbled up from deep inside her. "It's actually kind of funny, you know? I met David when I was sixteen. I was… well, let's just say I was trying to get his attention. I was dropping all the hints, making all the moves. And he was just… immovable." She laughed, a rich sound filled with years of understanding. "He'd just make excuses about being too young. It was incredibly frustrating, and oddly… endearing."

Sara, still cradling a very confused Jake in his carrier, looked from Josh to Tiffany, her brow furrowed. "So, he just… ignored you?" "No, not at all. He was always kind, funny and very committed, but always focused. Romance was… a lower priority, to say the least." Tiffany reached for a brush, gently working through the miniature cow's thick coat. "I eventually figured out why. He'd been heartbroken so many times in his previous life. A wife, a girlfriend... David knew it would be a distraction. He knew living this life with him was going to be unique and challenging. It requires sacrificing your own life to his vision."

Josh snorted, shaking his head. "Yeah, try telling that to some of the newer recruits. They still don't understand the… cooperation." He turned to Sara. "Not everyone's cut out to be David's wife, you know? It takes a special kind of patience... and a damn good sense of humor." Tiffany bumped Josh playfully with her hip. "Don't let it go to your head. I just had blind faith, fueled by curiosity. Plus a high tolerance for Jennifer's shenanigans." She sighed dramatically. "Anyway, Summer and Jennifer kind of popped in while I was in college, and we kinda formed this... triad. We're his support, his confidantes... not his distractions."

Sara tilted her head. "A triad? Like a... three-way sisterhood?" "It was rough in the beginning." Tiffany sighed, dipping her brush into a bucket of soapy water. "Looking at Jennifer, Summer... even Elena later on, you know, women who wanted the same thing as you, women who wanted your husband... It wasn't exactly comfortable." She paused, searching for the right words. "It was hard to smile. Hard to pretend everything was okay. Harder to believe it actually was okay."

Sara shifted Jake in his carrier, his little face scrunched up in an expression of utter bewilderment. "I... I can't even imagine sharing Marvin like that." "It's not for everyone," Tiffany conceded, her voice softening. "But David... he has a way of making you understand. He needs us. Not just physically, but emotionally, intellectually. We're his anchors, his confidantes." A tear traced a path down Tiffany's cheek, unnoticed at first as she focused on Tiny's coat. "He always reminded me of the only promise I ever asked him to keep," she whispered, her voice thick with emotion. "'Never forget me.'"

The tears started to flow freely now, a dam bursting after years of careful control. She dropped the brush with a clatter, turning away from Sara and Josh, burying her face in Tiny's surprisingly soft fur. "David made me more promises than I ever thought to ask," she choked out, her voice muffled by Tiny's fur. "He promised me safety, security, a future... a family. And he delivered on every single one. And still, sometimes, I feel like that sixteen-year-old girl, desperately trying to get his attention, falling head over heels all over again."

Josh, suddenly awkward, cleared his throat. "Hey, Tiff... you okay?" Tiffany sniffled, lifting her head and wiping her eyes with the back of her hand. "Yeah," she said, her voice shaky but determined. "Yeah, I'm okay. It's just... damn, I love that man. He's been through so much! He burdens himself with protecting everyone and everything! It's exhausting."

A watery smile touched her lips. "And if I could go back," she confessed, a mischievous glint returning to her eyes, "to that first moment I met David, I would have... well, let's just say I wouldn't have been so kind. I would have fucked him every single time I was with him!"

Josh burst out laughing, the sound echoing through the barn. Sara, still slightly dazed, managed a small smile. "Well, that's one way to get his attention," she said, shaking her head in amusement. "I still think he's a unicorn, honestly." Tiffany laughed, her voice still shaky. "He's no unicorn, Sara. He's just a man, with all the flaws and insecurities that come with it. But he's my man, and I love him more for it."

Sara looked at Tiffany with a mixture of curiosity and admiration. "What's the catch, then? It can't all be kept promises and great sex." "The catch, Sara," Tiffany began, her voice softening, "is David himself. His personality. He...

he requires constant assurance. And control. Not in a tyrannical way, not really. More like… if he doesn't feel like he's got a firm hand on the wheel, he shuts down."

She pushed off the cow, walking a few steps to stroke Tiny's bristly head. "You see, for David, responsibility isn't just a word. It's… it's his everything. He takes it so seriously. And if he's made responsible for something, for everyone here, and then you try to take away his control over it? To him, that's not just a challenge; that's betrayal. And David… he doesn't do betrayal."

Josh, who had been listening intently, nodded slowly. "So, if someone tried to undermine him, or reject him, he'd… just stop?" "Worse than stopping, Josh," Tiffany replied, turning to face them, her eyes serious now, though a faint, knowing smile played on her lips. "He would stop caring. He'd burn everything to the ground, metaphorically speaking, of course. Because for David, his entire sense of worth, his very identity, is wrapped up in being a good husband, a good father, a good leader. In taking care of all of us. If he feels like he's failed at that, or that he's unappreciated, or worse, unwanted… then what's the point? He'd lose his purpose, and that's a terrifying thing for a man like him."

Tiffany leaned against the Zebu, Rita, who responded with a low, contented rumble. "But despite all that intensity," she continued, a softer, almost wistful expression settling on her face, "he's actually a very easy person to love. And honestly, he's not difficult to figure out. The trick is, you just have to let him be David. Let him do what he does."

Sara paused, a sudsy cloth dripping in her hand. "So, we just… don't question him?" Tiffany chuckled. "Oh, you can totally question him! In fact, he wants you to question him, not in a challenging way, but in an 'I want to understand' way. He hates ambiguity, probably more than anything. If you ask him why he's doing something, he'll explain it, in excruciating detail if you let him. He wants you to understand his reasoning, his logic, his plans. He wants you to be on board, not just compliant."

Josh nodded, still methodically brushing Bruticus, whose thick hide seemed to absorb the bristles without complaint. "So, it's about understanding, not just obedience." "Exactly!" Tiffany beamed. "And here's the really beautiful part about him. David isn't some cookie-cutter provider, tossing out generic kindness. He doesn't treat everyone the same. He caters his love, his care, his affection to you. Based on what he sees, what he knows about you, and most importantly, what you tell him. He observes, he learns, and he adapts. He tries to give you what you need, what you want, in the way you would best appreciate it. He's like a five-star chef for emotional nourishment, always whipping up a custom dish."

She paused. "But there's a flip side to that, too. Because if he's gone to all that effort, if he's poured his heart and soul into providing for you, caring for you, giving you a gift, whether it's a physical thing, an opportunity, or even just his unwavering support, and if that person rejects his care or his gifts? Well, that's it. That's the end of it. You've rejected him. And David… he might never offer you anything like that again. Not really. He'll still provide for your basic needs, of course, because he's David, and that's his fundamental purpose; he's not going to let you starve or freeze. But that deeper, tailored, affectionate care? Poof. Gone like a fart in the wind, leaving only the essentials."

Sara shivered. "That's… intense." "It is," Tiffany agreed, her eyes twinkling with a mix of profound affection and an almost mischievous amusement. "Take this barn, for instance." She gestured grandly around the vast space. "It's my paradise, truly. I specifically asked David for a proper barn, a beautiful, functional space for the animals, a place where I could really connect with them. I wanted it. He built it. He poured his extraordinary mind and resources into making this exactly what I dreamed of, and then some. It has better heating and cooling than some of the old suburban McMansions."

She tilted her head, her smile widening into a playful grin. "Now, imagine if, after he gave me this magnificent structure, built exactly to my specifications, I turned around and accused him of forcing me to work on the ranch, or trying to 'win' at marriage by buying my affection with a fancy barn. Imagine if I spat on his efforts and rejected this place as some kind of burden or manipulation, saying something like, 'Oh, so now I have to groom the Zebu because you built me this big stable?' "

Josh and Sara waited, wide-eyed, for the punchline, captivated by Tiffany's dramatic delivery. "He wouldn't just be disappointed," Tiffany declared, her voice dropping conspiratorially, yet maintaining a light, almost gleeful tone.

"He might just… burn the whole damn barn down. With all the animals inside. Sara's jaw dropped, her hand stilling on Rita's glossy, dark coat. "He would… he would literally burn it down?" she whispered, her eyes wide with a mixture of horror and fascinated disbelief.

Josh, who had paused mid-brush stroke on Bruticus, let out a nervous chuckle. "Tiff, you're just trying to scare her, right? Dad wouldn't really do that. I mean, it's a barn. And a really nice barn, at that." He gestured with the brush. Tiffany leaned against the sturdy wooden railing of a stall, a faint, knowing smile playing on her lips. "Oh, I assure you, dear Josh, he absolutely would. And no, Sara, I'm not joking in the slightest." Her voice was still light, almost melodic, completely at odds with the severity of her words. "David's commitment, whether it's to a grand project or to a relationship, is absolute. He pours himself into it. He gives everything. And for him, to have that gift, that effort, that love thrown back in his face, disrespected, or worse, used as a weapon against him… well, that's an entirely different category of offense."

She paused, looking from Josh's bewildered face to Sara's still-shocked expression. "He wouldn't do it out of malice, mind you. Not out of anger in the way you or I might lash out. It would be… a severing. A profound statement of, 'If this is what you truly wish, if you want to invalidate all that I have given, then so be it.' He would see it as the only logical conclusion to such an act of rejection." Sara swallowed hard. "But… it would hurt him, right? To destroy something he built with so much care? And the animals?"

107

Tiffany nodded slowly, her smile softening into something more poignant. "It would hurt him terribly. More than it would hurt me, perhaps, in that moment. It would tear him apart, to dismantle something he had poured his being into, especially knowing that it was once a source of joy for someone he loved. But that, dear Sara," she said, her gaze distant for a moment, "that would be his burden to bear. The cost of my imagined betrayal. He would steel himself, do what he felt was necessary to excise the source of such profound disrespect, and then he would carry the weight of that deed. That's just who he is. His sense of justice, even when applied to himself, is unyielding."

She turned her attention back to Tiny, her movements deliberate and tender. "And with it, of course, our relationship, our trust... it would be lost, just as surely as the barn would be consumed by flames." Her voice dropped to a near whisper. "David would never, ever try to reach me in that same way again. The vulnerability, the openness, the willingness to build and share something so deeply personal... that would shatter. He wouldn't offer it, because he would understand that I had proven myself incapable of receiving it in the spirit it was given."

Josh, still trying to process the idea of his calm, collected father-in-law being capable of such a drastic act, ventured, "But he'd forgive you eventually, wouldn't he? Like, if you apologized?" Tiffany sighed, a soft sound, yet imbued with a lifetime of understanding. "Oh, he might. Eventually. David is capable of immense forgiveness. But it wouldn't be for a very, very long time. And even then, it would be a different kind of forgiveness. Not the kind that mends the original wound. Our relationship, as it exists now, the deep, abiding trust and partnership that allows for such magnificent gifts as this barn to be built and appreciated… that would be irrevocably broken."

She stroked Tiny's head, her eyes fixed on the small zebu. "It's why I cherish this barn so much. It's not just a structure, or a place for animals. It's a testament to his love, his dedication, and our mutual understanding. When he gives, he gives completely. And when I receive, I receive completely, with gratitude and respect. Because to do otherwise, to spit on that kind of dedication… well, you've seen what he's capable of building. Imagine what he's capable of un-building."

Josh stood there, the brush half-raised, his mind reeling. Tiffany's words, delivered with such quiet intensity, clicked into place like the final, crucial pieces of a puzzle he hadn't even realized he was solving. David, the patriarch who radiated calm authority and boundless affection, was also capable of such devastating, absolute withdrawal.

It made sense now. All the stories, the hushed whispers from the older women, the anecdotes about his own mother, Lynn. They painted a picture of a David far different from the one he knew. A David who, when Tiffany and Summer first stepped into his orbit, hadn't welcomed them with open arms, but with a wall of polite but unyielding rejection. Josh had always heard it as a sort of quirky, romantic pursuit, two young women chasing an elusive teenage boy until he finally relented. But Tiffany's explanation reframed it entirely. David wasn't playing hard to get; he was terrified to get.

He remembered fragments of conversations, hints dropped by Summer and Tiffany in unguarded moments. How David had seemed... broken from the start, despite his competence and strength. Not physically, but deeply, intrinsically. He hadn't just survived an apocalypse; he had survived something far more insidious. His entire first life, hadn't been destroyed by the apocalypse itself, the blackout, the chaos, the collapse, but by the insidious decay of his most intimate relationships. The rejection, the betrayals, the misunderstandings, the slow, agonizing erosion of trust with those he had loved most. He had a life, a future, only for it to crumble not externally, but from within, because the foundations of his personal connections had fractured. That was the true apocalypse for David, the one that left deeper scars than any world-ending event ever could.

Josh's arm, mid-stroke on Bruticus's thick hide, froze. The brush dangled precariously from his fingers. The foundations had fractured from within. He replayed Tiffany's words, slowly, like a broken phonograph record. "Imagine what he's capable of un-building." A cold dread trickled down his spine. This wasn't just about the ranch, the bunkers, the fortress David had meticulously constructed around them. This was about the fortress David had built around himself, against the very people who claimed to love him. It wasn't about protection from the outside world; it was protection from the inside.

And then, like a lightning bolt, it clicked into place with his own mother, Lynn. He'd always wondered why David, who seemed to have an endless wellspring of boundless affection for everyone else, particularly his wives, held Lynn at such a distance. It wasn't malice, never that. It was a polite, almost sorrowful detachment. Lynn, for her part, often tried a little too hard, her attempts at banter, her lingering glances, always met with David's cold shoulder. Josh had seen it as David being… David. A man of many attachments, but not that attachment. Now he understood. Lynn wasn't just someone David had been with; she was one of the initial cracks in that first life's foundation. The rejection from her, the mother of his own lost children, must have been a deep, festering wound.

Suddenly, a new image formed in his mind, replacing the abstract concept of fractured foundations with something oddly specific: a wedding cake. Not just any cake, but one of those ridiculously elaborate, multi-tiered monstrosities that required serious structural engineering to stay upright. David, in Josh's mental confection, was perched precariously on the very top, a tiny, almost doll-like figure, his arms outstretched, as if holding up the sky itself. But he wasn't holding the sky. He was being held.

The top tier, supporting David and all his grand, future-proof plans, rested on four sturdy pillars. These weren't fondant columns or plastic dowels. These were Tiffany, Jennifer, Summer, and Elena. The four women that helped carry his plan to fruition. In equal spacing, they stood on the middle tier, supporting the burden of David and his dreams. Below them, holding up the entire middle tier, were the other wives. Taylor, Nicole, Jessica, Kayla and Tanya. Also equally spaced apart, holding David's ranch above them, with the top tier securely on top.

The whole mental confection was absurd, yet it made perfect, undeniable sense. David wasn't merely the architect of this new world; he was its most precious, most vulnerable cargo, balanced atop a matriarchal structure of his own making. The women weren't just attracted to him for his intelligence or dominance or leadership; they were the very foundation that allowed that intelligence, dominance, and leadership to exist. They were the antidote to the internal fracturing. They were the ones who understood the true, deeper apocalypse David had survived, and they were, each in their own way, ensuring it would never happen again.

"You gonna brush that zebu all day, or are you just gonna stare at him?" Sara's voice cut through Josh's profound reverie. "Bruticus looks like he's about to start charging you for rent on his face."

Chapter 19:

The Forge and the Well

Aidan was perched precariously on a scaffold, the acrid smell of burning metal filling the air. Below him, the rhythmic thud of rocks being hammered into place provided a steady soundtrack to the morning's construction. "Hey Aidan!" Lynn yelled up, her voice carrying more playful sarcasm than disdain. "Think you could aim a little better with those sparks? I don't want my hair catching fire!" Aidan chuckled. "Sorry, Lynn! Just trying to get this roof done. Plus, we have hats for that, remember?"

"Yes, but a girl can have standards!" she shot back with a grin, ducking just in case another stray spark came dangerously close. "Say, where's that lovely wife of yours? Haven't seen Alissa all morning." Aidan paused, wiping sweat from his brow with the back of his hand. "She's in the nursery, I think," he replied, squinting down at her. "Said she was going to help Sara with the little ones. You know, Poppy, Jake, Tyler, and Lucas. A real baby convention going on."

Lynn raised an eyebrow, a mischievous glint in her eyes. "Four babies? All at once? That's a handful! You going to get roped into diaper duty later?" "Wouldn't surprise me," Aidan sighed dramatically, though a smile played on his lips. "Alissa's got this way of making you feel like you're missing out on the real fun if you don't help. Plus, Poppy's got that whole crew wrapped around her finger."

Behind him, Parker and Eric were engaged in a less glamorous but equally important task: burying two large galvanized steel tubes that would provide ventilation for the smithy. They looked like giant worms wriggling into the hillside. Down below, the constant playful banter of those working quickly turned into a chorus of laughter. Josh had apparently tripped, sending a small cloud of mortar dust over Lynn. "You did that on purpose!" Lynn accused, wiping her face with a kerchief. Josh simply smiled, earning a playful smack on the arm from Mark.

The sounds of rifle fire from the shooting range crackled through the morning air and seemed to keep Aidan in check, reminding him that this was no ordinary construction project. This was survival, community, and a little bit of crazy all rolled into one. Bonnie, along with all of David's wives, were honing their marksmanship skills. Grace and Lily, ever the responsible ones, acted as range safety officers, their serious expressions a stark contrast to the occasional whoop of excitement when someone hit a particularly challenging target.

Over at the shooting range, Jessica fanned herself dramatically with a tattered target. "Sweet baby Jesus, it's hot enough to fry eggs inside of a chicken!" she exclaimed, her voice carrying across the compound. "I swear, Satan's swinging his sweaty ball sack over this whole valley!" Summer chuckled. "Jessica, darling, some of the children might hear you." "Let them hear!" Jessica retorted. "Gotta educate 'em somehow. Besides, it's true! Where's Daddy? He should be providing us with lemonade and moral support, not letting us bake out here like potatoes!"

Suddenly, David appeared, as if summoned. He was carrying a large cooler, which he set down with a thud. "Did someone call for Daddy?" he asked, his gaze sweeping over his wives. "And did I hear someone complaining about the heat?" Jessica immediately perked up. "Daddy! You're a lifesaver! This weather is trying to kill me!

David chuckled, placing a hand on her shoulder. "Now, now, Baby. It's barely 8:00 am. The sun hasn't even reached its peak yet. And besides," he gestured towards the covered shooting area, "we have that lovely awning providing shade and those high-powered fans circulating the air. I hardly think it's that bad out here." Jessica pouted, crossing her arms. "Thank you, Daddy," she said, her tone dripping with sarcasm. "Instead of sweating between the devil's butt cheeks, we get to experience the breeze of his flatulence. Truly, a luxury!"

David raised an eyebrow, a hint of amusement dancing in his eyes. "Well, aren't you a ray of sunshine this morning?" He popped open the cooler, revealing ice-cold drink bottles and a small stack of frozen popsicles. "Anyone for some refreshment? We have blue raspberry, cherry, and...surprise!" He pulled out a single, olive-green popsicle. "Pickle flavored. I thought you might appreciate this, Jessica." Jessica wrinkled her nose in disgust. "Pickle? Daddy, are you trying to poison me? I'd rather deep throat a mortar launcher. Do you hate me today?"

Summer laughed, stepping forward to grab a water bottle. "Don't be dramatic, darling. I'll take the pickle one. I'm feeling adventurous today." She gave David a grateful smile. "Thank you, David. You always know how to take care of us." Nicole chimed in, "Yes, thank you, David. It is nice to have something cold to drink. Though, Jessica, I do agree, pickle does sound like an abomination."

David made his way towards the burgeoning Smithy, a second cooler heavy with refreshments in tow. The sounds of grunts, the clink of rocks, and the scrape of shovels filled the air as the men diligently worked on the walls. He could see Aidan's tall frame silhouetted against the rising structure, meticulously sliding in cement boards. "Alright, fellas! Water break!" David announced, his voice booming across the site. "Come and get it before Jessica starts complaining about the heat again and sucks all the cool air out of the atmosphere."

Aidan chuckled, wiping his face with a towel. "Speaking of Jessica, how's she holding up over at the range? I thought she was gonna melt into a puddle last week." "She's...managing," David replied. "Let's just say her vocabulary has started to include some rather colorful descriptions of solar radiation and the devil's asshole."

Kyle, familiar with the vocabulary, piped up, "Sounds like it's reaching the nineties already." He tossed a rock onto the growing pile, then sauntered over to the cooler. "What goodies do we have today, David? Hopefully nothing vegetable-flavored." "Just the usual," David replied, popping open the cooler. "Water, lemonade, and...ah, yes. Someone requested watermelon slices. Don't tell Jessica, or she'll accuse me of playing favorites."

Lynn ignored the banter and grabbed a water bottle. "Thanks, David. This is a lifesaver. I swear, I'm sweating more than a hooker in Sunday school." "Tell me about it," Josh added, reaching for a lemonade. "This humidity is killer. Makes a man wanna pack up and move to Antarctica."

Mark silently grabbed a water and nodded his thanks to David. Marvin, on the other hand, was still stacking rocks, seemingly oblivious to the break. "Marvin, son, take a break. You're gonna work yourself into an early grave," David called out. Marvin didn't even pause, his back to them. "I'm in a rhythm, David! Gotta keep the momentum going!" he shouted, hoisting another hefty rock.

David sighed good-naturedly. "Alright, Marvin, but don't say I didn't warn you. Besides, I brought watermelon." The effect was instantaneous. The rock slipped from Marvin's grasp with a thud, and he spun around, eyes wide. "Watermelon? You said watermelon?" He abandoned the wall entirely and charged towards the cooler, a grin splitting his face. Aidan chuckled, shaking his head. The promise of watermelon was a universal motivator, especially in this heat.

David turned his attention to Kyle, who was leaning against the growing rock wall, a thoughtful expression on his face. "Kyle, what's the progress on the stonework? Looking sturdy enough to keep those future piggies contained?" Kyle pushed himself off the wall, taking a swig of his water. "It's coming along, David. I'm aiming for something that looks… well, not factory-made, you know? Stacking these rocks, it's like cobblestone. Gives it some character, some history." He gestured to the uneven surface, the varied sizes and shapes of the stones. "Adds to the rustic charm. Makes it look like it's been here for a hundred years."

"Rustic charm?" Lynn snorted, wiping her face with a bandana. "Charm's not gonna stop a boar with a vendetta." "It's not just charm, Lynn," Kyle retorted, a hint of defensiveness in his voice. "It's structurally sound. I'm wedging them in tight, using the right mortar. It'll hold, trust me."

David clapped Kyle on the shoulder. "I trust you, son. You've got a good eye. And a good understanding of how things work. Just make sure we get plenty of concrete in there too." Kyle nodded, a hint of pride in his eyes. As David returned to the house, he pointed toward a bundle of solid steel bars leaning against a nearby pile of rocks. "These are for shelf supports. I'm hammering them in as the wall goes up. They'll be embedded in the mortar, giving it extra strength."

Aidan, intrigued, walked over, leaving the cement boards for a moment. "Shelf supports? What kind of shelves you planning on putting in a pig pen?" Kyle puffed out his chest a bit. "Not the pig pen, Aidan. The shelves are for the Smithy." He gestured around with a flourish, a touch of showman in his demeanor. "Once the walls are up and the roof's on, this entire building becomes my Smithy. Those shelves are for tools, materials, finished projects... everything!"

Aidan blinked, the gears in his engineer's brain whirring. "Oh, I get it. You're already planning the Smithy construction. Good call." Kyle smiled, "I know it's a temporary pig pen. But this whole setup is just to quarantine the wild pigs. Once the pigs are clean, it'll be disinfected and the Smithy can be used for it's true purpose".

Josh, who was busy mixing mortar with Mark in a wheelbarrow, looked up, his brow furrowed. "Metal spikes seem kinda risky for hogs, Kyle. Wouldn't wanna give them ideas. Last thing we need is a pig figuring out how to climb and escape." Kyle waved a dismissive hand. "They won't be able to reach the shelves. I'm hammering the steel bars in high enough that those porkers won't accidently impale themselves."

Mark then pointed to an open space in the floor without a concrete foundation. "What's that for?" Kyle proudly proclaimed, "This, gentlemen, is where the magic happens! This is where we'll build the forge!" Aidan raised an eyebrow. "You sure that's safe? Fire and all, inside a hole in the ground?" Kyle grinned, his eyes sparkling with excitement. "Relax, Aidan! I've thought of everything. See that pit? There's several feet of rock underneath, in case we ever have to flood it in an emergency. The forge will be built on top of it."

Mark, sweat beading on his forehead, paused from his mortar mixing to chime in. "Flood it? You're planning on flooding your smithy, Kyle? That sounds like a recipe for disaster, not craftsmanship." "It's a safety feature, Mark!" Kyle retorted, undeterred. "Besides, it's not like we're working with raw materials, mostly repurposed scrap metal. The flooding is the 'Oh Shit' button."

"Repurposed scrap metal?" Eric snorted from above, where he was burying a ventilation tube. "You mean old car parts and discarded rebar? Sounds like you're building a junkyard sculpture, not a forge." "Alright, alright," Kyle said, holding up his hands. "I admit, maybe I'm being a little... enthusiastic. But hear me out! We're not exactly working with virgin ore here, are we? Repurposed scrap metal is all we got for now. Gotta make do with what we have!" He hopped down into the pit, grabbing a handful of rocks. "And trust me, this ain't just some hole in the ground."

Lynn, emerging from behind a pile of rocks, adjusted her sunglasses. "Practically being the operative word, Kyle. I still don't understand why you need a flooding mechanism. Seems a bit extreme, even for you." Eric chuckled. "Yeah, what are you expecting, Kyle? A dragon to crawl out of the forge?" Kyle rolled his eyes. "It's not about dragons, Eric! It's about... contingency! What happens if something unexpected gets in there? A runaway fire fueled by who-knows-what? Toxic fumes from some weird alloy? I need a way to shut it down, fast! Think of it as the ultimate safety valve."

"Okay, okay, I get it," Lynn said, raising her hands in mock surrender. "Contingency. We get it, Kyle. You anticipate the worst. But flooding the whole place? What about rust? What about the mess? What about... everything?" She gestured wildly, encompassing the entire construction site. "It seems a bit much when fire extinguishers and a fire suppression system will work fine."

Kyle grinned, a hint of frustration shadowing his face. "Okay I was expecting that," he said, pointing an accusing finger at Lynn. "Fire extinguishers are great for surface fires, and the suppression system will help, but what if something starts smoldering deep within the forge itself? Coals can smolder for years if they're buried! This flooding system will quench everything in an instant. And to prevent excessive rust, that's why we have the pit, to drain out the excess water."

Mark, who'd been meticulously applying mortar like he was frosting a cake, piped up, "And what about the pigs, Kyle? You gonna flood the pigs?" Kyle stared at Mark, his jaw clenching. He took a slow, deliberate breath, trying to maintain his composure. He pointed his work glove at Mark, then at Eric, then back at Lynn. "Are you all just trying to piss me off? Is that the goal here? Because congratulations, you're succeeding!"

He grabbed his half-empty water bottle and slammed it down on a pile of rocks, the plastic crinkling under the force. "Look, I'm trying to build something useful here! But every single decision I make, every single idea I have, gets dissected and ridiculed! Do you think this is easy?"

His voice rose, echoing slightly in the quiet morning air. "I'm the one who has to figure this shit out! I'm the one who has to plan for every possible disaster! And all you can do is stand around and poke holes in my logic? Fine!" Kyle spat out the words like venom. "If you've got a better idea, then you build it! You design a better system! You deal with the rust and the mess and the goddamn pigs! I'm done!" "Fuck the Smithy, just build your goddamn pigpen," Kyle yelled, as he stomped away.

Josh exchanged a troubled look with Mark. He knew, better than most, how David would react to such constant questioning. It wouldn't be pretty. Aidan sighed, tossing his welding mask onto a nearby stack of cement board. "Alright, everyone just cool it for a minute. Let's let Kyle cool down. He's right, you know. He's putting in the work, the planning. A little less... criticism and a little more support wouldn't hurt."

Lynn, smoothing down her overalls, frowned. "I wasn't trying to be critical, Aidan. I just don't see the point of flooding it. Seems like a waste of water, that's all." "He said it was a safety measure," Mark countered, picking at a fleck of mortar on his fingernail. Eric scoffed, kicking a loose rock. "Using old car parts? Rebar? That's some MacGyver shit, man. He's gonna end up building a tetanus machine."

Josh spoke up, his voice low and deliberate. "You guys are missing the point. It's not about whether his ideas are perfect, it's about the constant... interrogation. You think David wouldn't lose it if we questioned every single decision he makes?" A hush fell over the group. The comparison to David hung heavy in the air. David's leadership, his vision, was rarely questioned. His word was law, and his decisions, while sometimes eccentric, were always respected, if not always understood.

Parker, wiping sweat from his bald head, shifted uncomfortably. "Alright, alright, Josh. Point taken. But Kyle shouldn't fly off the handle like that. We're all in this together." "I'll go talk to him," Aidan said, wiping his hands on his jeans. "Just... try to be a little more supportive, okay? Even if you don't understand his vision, try to see it from his perspective."

He started after Kyle, but as he stepped off the foundation, he saw a flash of movement leaving the range and running after Kyle. Grace, her lithe form a blur of motion, was already halfway to him, her silvery blonde hair flying behind her. He felt a pang of relief as she managed to slow Kyle down, even if he didn't stop. He knew that Grace had a unique understanding of Kyle, one that the rest of them couldn't quite grasp.

Turning back to the others, Aidan saw the awkward silence that had fallen over the group. He knew that they hadn't meant to offend Kyle, but their constant questioning and doubts had clearly taken a toll on him. Aidan took a deep breath and spoke up, "Alright, let's get back to work. We'll try to keep the questions to a minimum and focus on helping Kyle instead of hindering him. Lynn, maybe you can help Eric with the ventilation tubes? Mark, you can double-check the mortar mix. Josh, keep stacking those rocks. We need this Smithy built, and we need to do it together."

As the group got back to work, Aidan couldn't help but feel a sense of frustration building up inside of him. He knew that Kyle's ideas were unconventional, but he also knew that they were brilliant. The others just couldn't see it yet. Meanwhile, Kyle was fuming. Did they think he was an idiot? He had thought this through, every detail, every potential problem. He had a vision, a plan, and they were treating him like the new kid in the sand box.

Kyle had walked away, not out of anger, but out of sheer frustration. He needed to escape the suffocating atmosphere of doubt and skepticism. He needed to breathe, to clear his head, to remember why he was doing this in the first place. He didn't even register Grace falling into step beside him until they had walked quite a distance. He knew she was there, he could feel her presence, but his mind was too preoccupied to acknowledge her. He just kept walking, his boots crunching on the dry grass, his gaze fixed on the horizon.

When they reached the large boulder that concealed the entrance to the wellhouse, Grace stepped forward. Without a word, she put her shoulder to the rock and pushed, the heavy stone scraping against the ground as it moved aside. Then, she reached down, unlatched the hatch, and swung it open, revealing the dark, cool interior of the wellhouse. "It's cooler and there's shade down here," she said simply, her voice soft and gentle.

Kyle stopped, finally turning to face her. He looked at her, and saw the concern in her eyes. He saw the understanding, the empathy, the unwavering belief in him. He felt a knot in his chest loosen, the tension that had been building up inside him slowly dissipating. He nodded, a small, almost imperceptible movement. "Yeah," he said, his voice rough. "Yeah, it probably is."

Kyle lowered himself into the cool, damp darkness of the wellhouse, Grace following close behind. The air was a welcome contrast to the oppressive heat of the Texas sun. He sank to the ground, leaning his back against the curved wall, the coolness seeping into his sweaty shirt. He closed his eyes, trying to quiet the storm raging in his mind. Grace remained standing, her presence a silent reassurance. She didn't pry, didn't offer empty platitudes. She simply waited, allowing him the space he needed. He knew she understood, perhaps better than anyone else.

Kyle sighed, rubbing a hand over his face. "It's just…," he began, his voice low and gravelly, "it's like they think I'm an idiot. I know what I'm doing, Grace. I've thought this through. I've planned it for months." He gestured vaguely in the direction of the Smithy, his anger rekindling. "They act like I haven't built anything before. Like I don't know the first thing about forging or… or anything!"

He paused, taking a deep breath. "It's not just about keeping the pigs," he continued. "It's about having a place, a real place, where I can create. Where I can take scrap metal and turn it into something useful. Something useful, even." He looked up at Grace, his eyes searching hers. "Do you understand?" Grace nodded slowly. "I do, Kyle. I always have. That's why it bothers you so much, isn't it? They don't see it. They can't see past the rocks and rebar." She knelt beside him, her hand resting lightly on his arm. "They don't see the vision."

Kyle leaned his head back, closing his eyes. "It's not just that, Grace. It's… it's David. He trusted me with this. He gave me the freedom to…" "To build," Grace finished for him. "Exactly." A tense silence hung between them for a moment, Kyle's brow furrowed. "You think I'm being unreasonable?" Grace shook her head. "My dad would have lost it too. That's why he doesn't explain his projects halfway. Most people can't see the final product through the draft."

Grace squeezed his arm gently. "Just stop debating them, Kyle." He opened his eyes, looking at her with a mixture of surprise and confusion. "What?" "Stop trying to explain yourself. Stop trying to justify every decision. Just... build it." Kyle frowned. "But... David..." "David trusts you, Kyle," Grace interrupted, her voice firm. "He gave you this project because he knows what you're capable of. He doesn't need a detailed explanation of every brick and bolt."

Kyle considered her words, the gears turning in his mind. "But what if..." "What if they don't like it?" Grace finished, her voice laced with a hint of amusement. "So what? It's your Smithy, Kyle. Not theirs." "But they're all helping," he protested weakly. "They're putting in the work." Grace nodded. "They are. Their job is to stack rocks and dig dirt. Let Aidan build your roof and walls. If you need to add something, just do it."

After a short quiet moment, Grace shifted, straddling his lap and facing him. Her hands gently framed his face as she leaned in, her expression suddenly serious. Grace looked into his eyes. It was as if she was trying to convey a depth of feeling he struggled to comprehend. She leaned in, her lips brushing against his. The kiss was soft, tentative at first, then deepening with a sudden surge of passion. She pulled back slightly, her breath warm against his skin.

"This Smithy..." she whispered, her voice serious, "is going to be our family's legacy." "Legacy?" Kyle asked, trying to keep his voice steady. "I think the whole ranch is a bigger legacy, don't you?" Grace shook her head, her eyes sparkling with a fierce determination. "I'm not talking about David, Kyle. I'm talking about you and me. This Smithy... is something we create. It's going to be here long after we're gone. It's a testament to what we can build together."

She kissed him again, a longer, more lingering kiss that spoke of shared dreams and unspoken promises. As their lips parted, she whispered against his mouth, "Imagine our children, Kyle. Imagine our children teaching their children to forge steel in that very spot, to shape metal with their own hands, using the tools you designed."

Kyle swallowed, the image she painted suddenly taking shape in his mind. He saw it, his children, the children he and Grace would have together, inheritors of the skills and knowledge he passed down, standing at the forge, their faces illuminated by the firelight. An undeniable flame ignited within him, a purpose that went beyond simply building a functional structure.

Grace deepened the kiss, her hands moving to cup his face, her thumbs caressing his cheekbones. "They'll tell stories about their grandfather, the man who built the Smithy with his own two hands, the man who wouldn't let anyone tell him it couldn't be done."

Grace began to unbuckle her plate carrier, the heavy ceramic plates clattering softly on the ground as they were set aside. Then Grace removed her gun belt and placed it next to the plate carrier. She continued to kiss him, her fingers digging into his hair, urging him closer. Then, Grace removed her shirt, the soft fabric whispering against her skin as it slid down her arms and landed on the ground. The pale light filtering through the small opening at the top of the well house illuminated the smooth curve of her shoulders, the delicate line of her collarbone.

Grace pulled Kyle's face to her chest, his lips pressing against the top of her breasts, feeling the rapid thrum of her heartbeat against his lips. It was a sacred moment, a private communion in a world that had lost all sense of sanctity. Grace then removed Kyle's gun belt and shirt, setting them off to the side. The coolness of the concrete against his bare back was a grounding sensation, a reminder of the solid foundation upon which they stood.

She leaned back, her gaze locked on Kyle's. Then she reached behind her, her fingers fumbling for a moment before her bra unclasped, the lacy fabric placed softly atop the expansion tank. Grace's actions left no doubt about her intentions. Now on her knees, her eyes met Kyle's, a silent invitation. Kyle, usually the stoic, felt his jaw go slack.

"Woah, Grace," he managed, his voice a low growl. "Are… are we really gonna… do it in here?" Grace simply nodded, her gaze unwavering, and reached for the buckle of his pants. The snap of the buckle echoed in the confined space. Kyle sucked in a breath. As his jeans pooled around his ankles, Grace didn't hesitate. She gently pushed them further down his legs, then leaned forward, her movements sure and deliberate.

The feel of her lips sent a jolt through him that bypassed his brain entirely. He gripped the cold concrete wall behind him, trying to maintain some semblance of composure. "Grace," he gasped, his voice tight with a mixture of pleasure and incredulity. "This is... fuck! Grace, muffled against him, let out a hum that vibrated against his skin.

Kyle's mind floated. The well house, usually a place of mundane maintenance, had transformed into a surreal landscape of desire. Grace's lips parted, a burning desire in her eyes. Her tight jeans and boots were a bizarre juxtaposition to her bare torso, the lacy bra discarded like a forgotten battle flag. He ran a hand through her hair, the cool concrete against his back doing little to calm the inferno raging within him.

He watched her, a silent symphony of lust and disbelief playing out in his head. She was exquisite. The curve of her neck, the way the dim light played on her skin, the sheer audacity of the moment, it all coalesced into a vision of pure, unadulterated sexiness. He swallowed hard, his throat suddenly dry. "Grace," he breathed, his voice thick with a desire that threatened to overwhelm him. "You're... you're amazing."

Grace smirked, a hint of triumph in her expression. She stood, a slow, deliberate movement that only served to heighten the tension. She admired her handiwork, her gaze lingering on the evidence of his arousal. Kyle could only stare, a prisoner of her captivating beauty and his own overwhelming lust.

His cock throbbed, painfully so, a testament to her skill and his own barely restrained desire. Grace reached out, her fingers tracing the length of him, sending shivers down his spine. He groaned, unable to resist the wave of pleasure that washed over him. He watched, mesmerized, as she kicked off her boots, the thud of leather on concrete. Then, with a slow, deliberate slide, her jeans followed, pooling at her ankles. The sight of her completely naked against the rough concrete wall stole his breath. She was a living sculpture, a masterpiece of human form.

She leaned back against the cool surface, her expression daring him. Then, with a fluid motion, she lifted one leg, extending it straight up, her arm holding it perfectly vertical. The pose was both vulnerable and incredibly powerful, showcasing the lean muscles of her thigh, the delicate curve of her hip, her remarkable flexibility, a tantalizing glimpse of... everything.

The silence stretched, thick and suffocating. Finally, Grace spoke, her voice a predatory command. "Fuck me, Kyle. Now." Without a word, Kyle surged forward, drawn to her as if by an irresistible gravitational force. He pressed his body against hers, the coolness of the concrete a stark contrast to the burning heat that flared between them. His hands found her waist, gripping her tightly as he lifted her slightly, positioning her perfectly.

Their lips crashed together, a desperate, hungry collision of need and desire. His tongue plunged into her mouth, tasting the sweetness of her, the raw, untamed essence of their forbidden connection. The world narrowed, focusing solely on the feel of her skin against his, the frantic rhythm of their breaths, the overwhelming urgency that drove them.

He thrust into her, a primal, instinctive movement that elicited a sharp gasp from Grace. "Yes," she moaned, her voice barely audible against his lips. "Oh, God, yes." He drove deeper, each thrust fueled by the pent-up longing, the forbidden thrill of their connection, the sheer audacity of the moment. Grace met him thrust for thrust, her hands tangling in his hair, pulling him closer, demanding more. The rough concrete scraped against her back, but she didn't seem to notice, lost in the escalating intensity of their passion.

Back at the shooting range, Josh approached Lily. "What happened? Grace just took off all of a sudden." She asked, looking in the direction of the house. Josh shook his head. "Kyle got frustrated and kind of blew up. Rightfully so. I don't know where he went, but he didn't go in the house, I'm sure." "Is he going to be alright?" she asked, concern etched on her face. Josh shrugged. "Probably, especially if Grace caught up to him."

Chapter 20:

The Gunsmith's Fiancé

Life at David's ranch was, for the most part, predictable. Predictably hot, predictably busy, and predictably…well, let's just say David had a unique way of running things. Today's mission? Operation: Wife Number Four. Callie's crush on Junior wasn't the ranch's worst-kept secret. But his wives knew, and that was enough. The problem wasn't a lack of affection on Junior's part, he was unfailingly kind to everyone. The obstacle was far more concrete: square footage. Junior's apartment, number 13 in the apartment bunker, was a cozy love nest for him and his three wives, Emma, Riley, and Olivia. Cozy bordering on cramped.

But Callie was not one to be deterred by mere spatial limitations. She had a plan, a beautiful, audacious plan involving Apartment 15, currently gathering dust and cobwebs. All she needed was Aidan, the resident miracle worker, to transform the space into a suitable harem habitat.

As she approached the group in the main house, map spread out on the table, she felt a surge of affection. This felt like home, this…family. The ranch was a haven, and she yearned to be an even bigger part of it. Aidan straightened up, a welcoming smile crinkling the corners of his eyes. "Hey, Callie! What's up?" Tiffany chimed in, "Good afternoon, dear! You look like you're about to burst with energy. What's got you so excited?"

This casual acceptance, this effortless inclusion, only fueled Callie's desire to belong. See? They were already treating her like family! "Afternoon!" Callie chirped, her voice brimming with excitement. "I was just thinking...about Apartment 15." Aidan raised an eyebrow, intrigued. "Apartment 15? What about it?"

Before she could launch into her meticulously rehearsed speech, her eyes landed on the young woman pressed against Kyle's side. She was pretty, with long, almost silvery-blonde hair and an air of quiet confidence, but something about her was...off. She carried herself with the maturity of an adult, yet her face held the smooth, undefined quality of a teenager, and her frame was slight, her hips lacking the gentle curve of womanhood. Callie had seen her around with Kyle before, always clinging to his arm, and had simply filed her away as his fiancée. It made sense; in this new world, people coupled up young.

Deciding to be polite before getting down to business, Callie beamed at the couple. "Sorry to interrupt what looks like very important piglet-plotting," she said with a wave at the map, where Kyle was circling a potential nesting area for a feral sow. "I should introduce myself properly! I'm Callie." She extended a hand to the young woman. "You must be Kyle's fiancée. It's so nice to meet you!" The young woman's eyes, a startlingly intelligent shade of blue, met hers. A warm, genuine smile spread across her face as she took Callie's hand. Her grip was firm, confident. "It's nice to meet you too, Callie. I'm Grace."

Callie's mental gears whirred for a split second. Grace? She'd heard that name before. Nicole's daughter. The fifteen-year-old twin. But that couldn't be right. This woman was clearly in her early twenties, at least. And she was with Kyle, a man in his thirties. The ranch was a big place, with over fifty people now. It stood to reason there was more than one Grace. It was a common enough name. Mystery solved. "Grace! What a pretty name," Callie gushed, relieved to have sorted it out in her head. "That must be a popular name here. I was so confused for a second! I was like, wait a minute, the timeline isn't adding up!" She laughed, a bright, bubbly sound that echoed in the kitchen.

Grace's smile didn't waver, though a flicker of amusement danced in her eyes. She exchanged a quick, knowing glance with Kyle, who simply shook his head, a ghost of a smirk on his face, before tapping a point on the map. "Yes, it is," Grace replied smoothly, her voice sweet and even. She released Callie's hand, turning her attention back to Kyle. She leaned in, kissed his cheek softly, and pointed to a different spot on the map. "They won't nest that close to the creek bed, the soil's too damp. Check this ridge line instead. It offers better cover from predators and a clear line of sight."

Her tone was so certain, so knowledgeable, that Callie was momentarily taken aback. This Grace was clearly very smart. Callie filed that fact away next to 'Kyle's Fiancée' and refocused on her primary mission. Aidan, who had watched the entire exchange with a look of profound, silent amusement, finally cleared his throat. "So, Callie," he prompted. "You were saying something about Apartment 15? You had some thoughts?"

"Oh! Yes! My thoughts!" Callie clasped her hands together, her energy returning in a rush. "Okay, so you know how Apartment 15 is right next door to Junior's, Apartment? And you know how it's currently empty, just sitting there, full of potential and lonely furniture?" She didn't wait for an answer. "Well, I was thinking, and you told me it was structurally possible, what if we knocked down the shared wall between the living rooms? We could combine them!"

Aidan leaned against the granite countertop. He crossed his arms, a slow, indulgent smile spreading across his face. "Okay, Callie," he said, his voice laced with a patient amusement he usually reserved for explaining a carburetor to a novice. "Walk me through this. You want to... knock down the wall." "Exactly!" Callie beamed, her whole body vibrating with the brilliance of her idea. She used her hands to frame a large, imaginary hole in the air between the refrigerator and the pantry. "Like, BAM! Open concept! Think of the flow! Junior needs space, Aidan. Plus, three wives! That's a lot of people in the standard apartment."

Tiffany, who had been quietly sipping her coffee and enjoying the entertainment, set her mug down with a soft clink. "He certainly is a busy young man," she agreed, her eyes twinkling. "And busy men need their space to unwind." She shot a knowing look at her son, a look that said 'play along, this is adorable'.

Kyle let out a low, rumbling chuckle. Grace glanced at him, a small smile touching her own lips before turning her observant eyes back to Callie. "Right? Tiffany gets it!" Callie pointed a finger at her for emphasis. "It would be like a real suite! A presidential suite! For our night-shift president! And with Apartment 15 being empty, it's the perfect opportunity."

Aidan held up a hand, a gesture for calm. "Okay, okay, I love the enthusiasm. But let's get technical for a second." He grabbed a napkin and a pen from a nearby holder. "Humor me. Let's draw this out." He sketched two rough rectangles side-by-side on the napkin. "This is Apartment 13, Junior's place. And this is Apartment 15, the empty one." Callie leaned over the counter, peering at his drawing, her brow furrowed in concentration.

"Now, every apartment has the same floor plan," Aidan continued, his pen tracing the layout. "Main door here, opens into the common room and kitchenette. Master bedroom down here, and the two smaller bedrooms are on this side." He pointed to the wall they shared. "So, the wall you want to knock down... see here?" He tapped the line between the two apartment drawings. "The one on the left of the living room and master bedroom of 15... "Yeah?" Callie urged, leaning closer. "...is right up against the back wall of Junior's two smaller bedrooms," Aidan finished, drawing a line through the imaginary bedrooms. "And this part," he tapped another section, "this is the main access corridor for the entire level. So your 'BAM! Open concept' would open up into a hallway and two tiny bedrooms, basically."

Callie stared at the crude drawing, her expression a mix of confusion and devastation. "So... Junior would walk through his living room and trip into a hallway?" "Essentially, yes," Aidan said, trying to sound gentle. Tiffany, who had been watching the exchange with maternal amusement while sipping her coffee, patted Callie's arm. "It was a nice thought, honey. Very generous."

"But it's for Junior!" Callie insisted, her spirit refusing to be completely crushed. "He and his wives deserve more space! They're crammed in there. Riley's always complaining she can't find a quiet corner to read. And what if they want kids? Where would they go?" She looked at the napkin again, a spark reigniting in her eyes. "Okay, okay, new plan. What if... we close this area off and build a wall there?" She jabbed a finger at the cubby between the apartments. "Then they get a super, mega, ultra living room!"

Aidan sighed, pinching the bridge of his nose as he visualized her new, equally chaotic blueprint. "Callie... then he would have two separate living rooms, separated by a kitchenette. It'd be like having two different houses connected by a pantry." Callie's face fell again. "Oh. That's... less palace-y." Aidan finally took pity on her. He folded her napkin blueprint and tucked it into his pocket before pulling a rolled-up sheet of drafting paper from a tube leaning against the island. He spread it out, revealing a clean, professional, and vastly more complex floor plan.

"I've actually already drafted a viable plan to combine apartments 13 and 15," he said, his tone shifting from patient friend to competent engineer. Callie's jaw dropped. "You have?" "Dad and I talked about it last month. Junior's family is the biggest single unit on the compound. It makes sense to expand their living space. It's just a matter of logistics and timing." He pointed to the professional drawing. "Your instincts were right, but the execution was... creative."

He traced a line on the blueprint. "The access to the main corridor for Apartment 15 could be closed off, and the entirety of both apartments could be enclosed into a single, cohesive unit. This is the key. You don't just knock down one wall." He swept his hand across the two apartment layouts. "Inside both apartments, every single wall would have to come down. They're modular, just framing and drywall inside the concrete shell. It's a gut job."

Callie stared, mesmerized, as he pointed out the new features. "Once we strip them to the bones, I can reframe it into one contiguous 1370-square-foot apartment. We'd go from four tiny bedrooms and two small ones to three much larger master suites, each with a walk-in closet. I'd be able to expand the kitchenette into a full galley kitchen and create one massive common room, three hundred square feet."

Callie was speechless, her eyes wide with awe. She looked from the elegant, detailed blueprint to Aidan's focused expression. A slow blush crept up her neck. "So... it can be done," she whispered. "It can be done," Aidan confirmed. "It's a big job. Junior and his family would have to relocate to another apartment for probably two weeks while we do the renovation. But it's entirely possible." Tiffany beamed, placing a fresh plate of vegetables in the center of the island. "That's my boy. Always one step ahead."

The confirmation snapped Callie out of her stupor, and her effervescent personality surged back to the forefront. "Two weeks? That's nothing! They could bunk with me! Oh my gosh, when can we start? Can we start tomorrow? We could have the demolition done by Friday!" she chirped, practically bouncing on the balls of her feet.

Aidan chuckled, rolling up the blueprints with practiced ease. "Hold on, energizer bunny. I appreciate the enthusiasm, but we have a few other things in the pipeline that take priority." He leaned against the counter, crossing his arms. "First, we have to finish the Smithy." "But it's built, isn't it?" Callie asked, her brow furrowing slightly. "I saw the structure go up."

"The structure is up, yes," Aidan clarified. "But it's not finished. We still have to use the backhoe to move all that earth and rock we excavated from the hillside and pack it against the east and west walls. The whole point is for it to be earth-sheltered, hidden from view from the main road and providing natural insulation. That's a few days of solid work right there."

As if on cue, Kyle, who had been listening quietly, spoke up. "And then there's the barn." Aidan nodded at him. "Exactly. We need to build the addition for the wild pigs we're planning to trap. We can't just throw them in with our current livestock. The Smithy is our quarantine zone, but after that, they need their own dedicated, reinforced pen attached to the barn."

Callie's face, which had been alight with the promise of her grand renovation project, began to cloud over. "Okay, okay, I get it," she said, her bubbly tone deflating ever so slightly. She tapped a finger nail on the countertop. "Pigs. They're important. But how long do they even have to be...

139

you know… pig-jailed for?" She waved a hand. "Like, a week? Two tops?"

Tiffany slid a bowl of sliced cucumbers next to the carrots and chuckled softly. "A little longer than that, sweetie. For new livestock, especially wild ones, you're looking at a quarantine period of about three months." She gave Callie a warm, knowing smile. "We have to be absolutely sure they're not bringing any diseases in that could wipe out the animals we already have. It's for the protection of our entire food supply."

Callie's eyes widened. "Three months?" The cogs in her brain were visibly turning, sparks of frantic calculation flying. Her face suddenly lit up again, her previous gloom forgotten in a flash of inspiration. "Wait! That's perfect! That actually works in our favor!" Aidan sighed, a fond, exasperated smile playing on his lips. He leaned back against the counter, ready for the inevitable rollercoaster of Callie's logic. "Alright, I'll bite. How does a six-month quarantine help you get Junior's apartment renovated tomorrow?"

"Look!" she announced, pointing a finger at Aidan, then Tiffany, then Kyle, as if conducting a symphony of brilliance. "You said burying the Smithy will take a few days. So, we do that! We all pitch in, get it done by, say, Monday, while you trap your pigs. Then you stick them in the newly-finished, super-quarantined Smithy. While they're in there, we start the apartment! Demolition, framing, drywall… Aidan, you said it would take two weeks! We'd be done before the middle of July! The pigs will still have over two months left in their quarantine jail. That gives us all of August and part of

September to build their fancy barn-condo before they need to move in. See?" She beamed, radiating triumphant confidence. "Problem solved. We can have it all!"

Just as Aidan was preparing a logical breakdown of all the potential flaws, a quiet voice cut through the doubt. It was Grace, who had been observing with her usual calm intensity. "That... actually sounds like a really good plan," she said, offering Callie a small smile. She pointed out that the timeline worked and the tasks were structured in a way that wouldn't drain their resources if managed properly.

Grace's endorsement was the turning point. Callie, beaming, seemed to gain a new wave of confidence. For Aidan, this was the moment the plan shifted from a hopeful wish to a practical possibility. As the resident engineer, his mind began to race, breaking down the complex proposal into its core components. Project 1: Earth-sheltering the Smithy. Project 2: Renovating an apartment with modular construction. Project 3: Building a new pig enclosure.

Pacing the length of the kitchen island, he analyzed Callie's timeline, her "critical path." Logistically, it was sound. The materials were available, and the machinery was ready. The biggest variable wasn't concrete or steel; it was morale. How could they keep everyone, especially the weary night shift, motivated for such a massive undertaking? The answer was standing right in front of him.

A slow grin spread across Aidan's face. "Alright, Callie," he announced, his tone shifting from skeptical to decisive. "You've sold me. The plan is a go." A squeal of joy erupted from Callie, but Aidan held up a hand. "On one condition," he said seriously. "This was your idea. Your passion. You just laid out a multi-stage construction schedule for the next three months. You know what that makes you?"

Callie blinked, her celebration paused. "Um… a genius?" she offered hopefully. Aidan chuckled. "It makes you the Project Manager," he declared. The weight of the title hung in the air. "You will be in charge of coordinating labor, making daily schedules, and acting as the official liaison for the crews. You want this, now it's your responsibility to lead it."

Her initial shock, a mix of terror and awe, quickly gave way to a surge of pure excitement. This was terrifying, yes, but it was also perfect. "You're not kidding?" she whispered, wide-eyed. "I never kid about a project timeline," Aidan confirmed with a grin. He then gave her her first official assignment: "I want you to draw up a volunteer roster for the Smithy project and talk to Noah, he's got a diorama of the ranch, so he's the perfect person to design its camouflage."

With that, a new leader was born, not by appointment, but by passion. As Aidan put it, "Welcome to management, Callie. Now, if you'll excuse us, we have some pig-napping to finalize."

He turned back to the small group at the massive granite island. Aidan pointed a finger at a map of the ranch laid out on the counter. "So, the primary trap zone will be here, northeast of the Smithy. Kyle, you and Scott can do the final scout tomorrow at dawn. Grace, I want you to go over the feed composition with Nicole one more time. We want them docile, not comatose." She nodded seriously. "I'll cross-reference it with the wild-foraging guide. Some native berries have a calming effect," she said, her voice soft but clear. Wow, she knows her stuff, Callie thought, impressed. Botany, animal husbandry... she's probably a genius.

The meeting broke up. Tiffany came over and gave Callie's arm a gentle squeeze. "Congratulations, dear. David always says passion is the best engine for progress." "Thanks, Tiffany! I feel like I just drank a gallon of coffee and got struck by lightning!" Callie beamed, bouncing on the balls of her feet.

As Tiffany moved towards the living room, Callie saw her opening. Kyle and Grace were gathering the map, their movements easy and familiar. This was her chance. As Project Manager, she was still getting used to the thought, she needed to build relationships. And this woman, this brilliant, kind-looking fiancée of the head gunsmith, seemed like a perfect place to start.

She took a deep breath, puffed out her chest with a newfound sense of purpose, and strode over, a wide, friendly smile plastered on her face. "Hey! Sorry to interrupt! That pig-trapping plan sounds amazing. Super organized!" Kyle gave a small, appreciative nod. "Aidan runs a tight ship." He looked down at Grace, his expression soft. "But this one's the real brains of the operation."

Callie's smile widened. "Well, you're obviously brilliant. The botany stuff? The animal psychology? My brain would just pop." Grace offered a gentle, polite smile. She had a calm, centered energy that was the complete opposite of

Callie's fizzy, chaotic vibe. "It's nice to meet you officially, Callie. I've heard your name around."

"You have?" Callie preened a little. "Well, as part of my… managerial duties… I'm trying to get a better handle on everyone's roles here. You know, for resource allocation and stuff!" She said the words like they were important and expensive. "So, what is it you actually do on the ranch, besides being a genius with pig tranquilizers? And how long have you been here? You seem like you've been a part of this place forever."

Grace's eyes flicked to Kyle for a split second, a flicker of amusement passing between them before she turned her serene gaze back to Callie. She knew exactly what Callie was thinking, that she was another one of the rescued adults, probably in her early-to-mid-twenties, settled comfortably into life with Kyle. She decided to have a little fun with it, without telling a single lie.

"I've been on the ranch for a while now," Grace began, her voice maintaining its soft, even tone. "Pretty much as long as I can remember, really." Wow, Callie thought. She must have been one of the very first people David welcomed. A true veteran. Grace continued, "As for my primary job… it's not really animal feed." She paused, letting the statement hang in the air. "My main function is scouting, infiltration, and intelligence collection."

Callie's jaw went slack. The bubbly energy in her chest was momentarily silenced by a wave of awe. "Infil… like… like a spy?" she whispered, her eyes wide. Kyle smirked, tightening his arm around Grace's shoulder. "She's the best

144

we have. No one sees what she sees." Grace gave a slight, self-effacing shrug. "I'm good at what I do. I also read lips," she stated simply. Callie instinctively snapped her mouth shut, realizing she'd been mouthing the word 'wow' over and over. Grace's lips quirked in a tiny smile. "I also have a deep understanding of kinesics and psychology. Body language. It's amazing what people will tell you without ever saying a word.

Motivation, for instance, is incredibly easy to spot if you know what to look for." Callie swallowed hard, suddenly feeling like she was made of glass. "Motivation?" she croaked. "Mmm," Grace hummed, her eyes holding Callie's with an unnerving placidity. "Take you, for example. I can see why you're so determined to prove. It's smart." She tilted her head slightly. "After all, if Junior gets a larger apartment, you have a much better shot at becoming his fourth wife."

The world stopped. The hum of the lights, the clink of Tiffany's cleaning cloth, Aidan's breathing, it all faded into a roaring silence in Callie's ears. Her crush on Junior wasn't a secret, exactly, but it was her thing. A hopeful ambition she nurtured in the dead of night while surveying the very Smithy she was now responsible for hiding. This woman, this super-spy, hadn't just seen her; she'd dissected her, analyzed her motives, and laid them bare on the kitchen counter like butchered meat. Her cover wasn't just blown; it was annihilated.

Her mind raced, trying to process the breach. How? When? Did Aidan tell her? Did she read my diary? I don't even keep a diary! She stared at Grace, this master of espionage, trying to pinpoint when she could have possibly been under such intense scrutiny.

Her brain scrambled for data, for any interaction, any shared space. She pictured Junior's three wives, Emma, Olivia, and Riley. Their loyalty, their connection to him. Did they talk? She thought about the last big community event... the ceremony. It was about three months ago, on the front porch. Junior was formally giving his wives their collars. It was a serious, intimate affair, but David had insisted on music to make it a celebration.

As Callie's mind replayed the scene, Junior's proud stance, the glint of silver in the evening light, the reverent quiet of the observers, a sound surfaced in her memory. A rhythm. A steady, complex, powerful beat that followed the event. There was a small, band set up to the side: Brian on a keyboard, Aidan and Seth on guitar, Lily on the Bass and a drummer.

Her memory zoomed in on the drummer. A figure sitting behind a well-worn drum kit, head down in concentration, sticks a blur of practiced motion. The drummer had been phenomenal, driving the music with a skill that seemed far beyond an amateur. Callie remembered looking over and being surprised by how... young the drummer was. A kid, really. A teenager with a sharp, focused face...

A spoon slipped from Tiffany's hand and clattered onto the granite countertop. The sharp, percussive sound snapped Callie's mental picture into razor-sharp focus. The drummer's face. The spy's face. They were the same. The realization hit Callie with the force of a physical blow. That wasn't Kyle's twenty-something spy fiancée. That was Grace. Grace! Nicole's daughter. Seth's twin sister. The sweet, quiet girl who was always with her brother or shadowing Kyle. The fifteen-year-old girl who had played drums at the ceremony.

Every ounce of air rushed from Callie's lungs. The awe she'd felt moments before curdled into a thick, hot wave of pure mortification. She hadn't been expertly profiled by a peer. She had been read like a children's picture book by a teenager. A teenager who was now looking at her with that same, placid, all-knowing smile.

Her eyes darted from Grace to Kyle and back again, her mind racing, trying to recalibrate this terrifying new reality. This wasn't just a simple May-December romance. This was… a power play of epic proportions. This fifteen-year-old girl, this quiet, observant musician, hadn't just caught the eye of one of the most capable and eligible men on the entire ranch. No. Callie's mortified, wildly imaginative brain knew this was a calculated move. Grace hadn't just snagged him; she had executed a flawless, long-term acquisition of a key strategic asset. Kyle, the gunsmith, the seasoned firearms expert, was now aligned with this… this Machiavellian prodigy in a teenager's body. Callie felt a cold sweat prickle her hairline.

The conversation about wild pigs faded into a meaningless buzz. Aidan was talking about feed ratios now, but Callie couldn't hear him. All she could see was Grace's calm expression, an expression that no longer looked sweet, but terrifyingly composed. "What," Callie blurted out, her voice a reedy whisper that cut through Aidan's sentence about corn versus protein pellets. Aidan, Tiffany, and Kyle all turned to look at her. "What was that, Callie?" Tiffany asked, her brow furrowed with motherly concern.

Callie's eyes were locked on Grace. "What do you want from me?" Aidan blinked, looking utterly bewildered. "From you? We were talking about pigs." "Not you," Callie breathed, taking a half-step back as if warding off an unseen force. Her gaze was intense, terrified. She was addressing Grace, and only Grace. "You. What is your angle? Your... your game?"

Kyle's lips twitched, the corner of his mouth threatening a full-blown grin. He'd seen people underestimate Grace before, but this was a new level of spectacular misinterpretation. Grace, for her part, didn't flinch. Her calm smile remained, her bright eyes holding Callie's gaze without a hint of malice. She tilted her head, a gesture of genuine curiosity. "I'm sorry?" she asked, her voice soft and even. "I don't understand."

The simple, polite question only fueled Callie's paranoia. It was a classic deflection. A master manipulator's opening gambit. "Don't play dumb with me," Callie whispered, leaning back slightly. "You're no ordinary kid. You saw right through me. You knew everything. Now you're standing here, with him," she gestured wildly at Kyle, "and you're planning... something. So just tell me. What's the price? What do I have to do?"

Kyle finally let out a low chuckle, unable to hold it in any longer. "Easy there, Callie. She's not recruiting for a shadow government. She just pays attention." But Grace held up a hand, silencing him gently. She looked directly at Callie, her expression softening from placid amusement to something warmer, something that looked suspiciously like empathy. The all-knowing smile remained, but its edges were kind. "I just thought," Grace said, her voice dropping to a conspiratorial level that mirrored Callie's own, "that we should be friends."

Callie stared, dumbfounded. Her brain, which had just constructed an elaborate espionage thriller, ground to a screeching halt. "...Friends?" The word came out as a squeak. "Yeah. Friends," Grace confirmed with a small nod. Her eyes flickered for a nanosecond towards the work shed, in the general direction of Apartment 13, where Junior lived. The movement was so subtle Callie almost missed it, but Grace knew she hadn't.

Then, Grace leaned in a little closer, her smile turning sly and helpful. "I could even help you," she added, her voice a sweet, quiet promise. "With your... goals." The silence that followed was monumental. Aidan was staring at the two of them as if they'd both started speaking fluent Russian. Tiffany was now smiling, a deep, knowing smile that said she understood everything perfectly. Kyle was just shaking his head, thoroughly entertained.

Callie was frozen, trapped between abject terror and a sudden, bizarre surge of hope. She had been seen, analyzed, and utterly dismantled by a fifteen-year-old girl. And that

same girl was now offering to be her wingman. She didn't
know whether to run for the hills or ask for a business card.

Chapter 21:

The Project of Affection

Under the glare of portable work lights, a scene of bizarre, post-apocalyptic industry was unfolding. Callie, armed with a clipboard that felt both like a scepter of power and a flimsy shield, stood watching. The ranch's backhoe, a monstrous yellow contraption, groaned and roared as it clawed at the dry earth, its fumes mingling with the scent of baked dirt and brittle grass. This was her project. Her first big one.

As project manager, Callie was trying her best to exude an aura of confident authority. She'd put on her most serious-looking cargo pants and tied her bubbly, blonde hair back in a tight, no-nonsense bun. Inside, however, her stomach was doing more acrobatics than the backhoe's articulated arm. "A little more to the left, Caleb! The west-facing berm needs a more aggressive initial gradient!"

The voice, calm and precise, belonged to Noah, who was standing overhead, watching the entire operation. He was holding his model, checking the finished plan, before looking up to direct Caleb, who was wrestling with the backhoe's controls. Callie bit her lip to keep from laughing. Noah, who could put a round through a keyhole at five hundred yards, was now a landscape architect, and his primary tool was a diorama that looked like an elaborate museum piece.

Caleb gave a thumbs-up from the cab. He loved the backhoe. He treated it like a giant Tonka truck, and his scoops of earth were always a bit more enthusiastic than strictly necessary. He swung the arm, dumping a mountain of dirt with a percussive thump that shook the ground. "Is that aggressive enough for ya, man?" Caleb yelled over the engine's rumble. "The slope is functionally adequate, but aesthetically, it lacks subtlety!" Noah called back, completely serious.

Callie sighed, tapping her pen against her clipboard. "Guys!" she shouted, her voice bright and cheerful, cutting through the masculine intensity. "David's notes just say, 'Make it look like a hill.' Minimal thermal signature, good water runoff. Let's not overthink the aesthetics. We're burying a building, not competing for the cover of Better Bunkers and Gardens."

A shadow fell over her, and Callie jumped, letting out a small squeak. "Sorry," came a quiet voice. It was Grace, of course. The girl moved with an unnerving silence that was both a gift and a minor cardiac threat to everyone else. "Grace! Don't do that!" Callie gasped, clutching her chest. "I'm going to make you wear a damn bell."

Grace offered a small, sweet smile, holding out two bottles of water. She handed one to Callie. "I thought you might be thirsty. Noah's been talking about 'occidental gradients' for twenty minutes. I figured you needed a break." "You are an angel sent from a much quieter, less pedantic heaven," Callie sighed, twisting the cap off the bottle and taking a long drink. The water was blissfully cold. "Thank you. Seriously. Is he always like this?"

Grace nodded, her eyes twinkling with amusement. "Seth often works with him on scouting patrols. He says Noah is usually a little too serious to be taken seriously. You just have to nod and agree that the dirt needs more character." Callie laughed. "Noted. Your brother has the patience of a saint." She took another sip of water, her mind shifting gears. She looked at Grace, this quiet, observant girl who seemed to navigate the complex social dynamics of the ranch with effortless precision. "Speaking of patience and getting what you want… how on earth did you do it?"

Grace tilted her head, her expression one of innocent curiosity. "Do what?" "Convince Kyle to be your fiancé," Callie said, lowering her voice conspiratorially. "I mean, he's… Kyle. He's a good guy, great with firearms, but he's also thirty-two and kind of… set in his ways. He's not one of David's boys, but still a pretty interesting pull, especially for a woman your age. Did you just sort of… declare him yours? And he went with it!" A serene, almost calculating, look crossed Grace's face. She took a delicate sip of her water before answering, her voice as calm and steady as a lake at dawn. "Oh, no. It wasn't a declaration. It was a long and arduous campaign."

Callie leaned in, completely captivated. "A campaign? Do tell. Give me the tactical debriefing." "Well, phase one was proximity and value demonstration," Grace explained, as if outlining a project plan. "I made sure my chores and his work schedule overlapped. When he was cleaning rifles in the

153

work shed, I'd be there organizing ammunition stores. I learned every component of every firearm he specializes in. I didn't just bring him coffee; I brought him the correct solvent for cosmoline removal without him having to ask."

Callie chuckled, shaking her head. "Okay, so you became indispensable. Smart. What was the next phase?" "Overcoming objections," Grace said simply. "The most difficult part was getting him over that last hurdle. It wasn't necessarily the age difference in general, people don't get too hung up on that anymore, but my chronological age in particular. Being fifteen was the primary roadblock." "How'd you manage that?" Callie asked, fascinated. "Did you have your dad talk to him?"

Grace shook her head, a small, knowing smile playing on her lips. "David's approval was a necessary condition, but it wasn't sufficient on its own. Kyle needed to see my maturity as genuine, not just an inherited echo of Dad's knowledge. My skills were never in question. He needed to see a wife, not just a skilled partner." "A wife," Callie repeated, testing the word. "So, less 'tactical asset,' more... what? Domestic goddess?"

"More like a partner in life, not just in survival," Grace clarified. "I started focusing on the things he didn't know he needed. I learned he hates the quiet after a long day at the range, so I made sure there was soft music playing in his apartment when he came back. I noticed he never took the time to make himself a proper meal, he'd just grab rations, so I started cooking for him. Not just sustenance, but his favorites. I learned he gets tension headaches, so I researched

154

massage techniques from one of Seo-Yeon's books. I created a sanctuary for him, a place where he wasn't just Kyle, the gunsmith, but just… Kyle." She paused, her gaze distant for a moment. "I listened. When he was frustrated with a difficult repair or worried about a patrol, I was there. I wasn't a child seeking reassurance; I was his confidante, his partner, his peace."

Callie was floored. This wasn't a teenage crush; it was a masterclass in emotional resource management and strategic partnership-building. It was beautiful, slightly terrifying, and utterly brilliant. "Grace, that's… that's a full-scale hearts-and-minds operation." She leaned forward again, her voice dropping. "Okay, so you secured the objective. How far has the… uh… post-campaign integration gone? Have you two… you know?"

Grace's sweet smile didn't falter in the slightest. There was no blush, no girlish hesitation. "Oh, absolutely," she said, as matter-of-factly as if discussing crop rotation. "Callie, look at our world. Wasting opportunities for happiness, for connection… for intimacy, is a luxury we can't afford. We have sex as often as we can." She took another sip of water. "Almost every night for the past week or so, he's come home exhausted. So, I make him dinner, I run him a hot bath, I lay out his pajamas, I suck his dick, and after I clean the kitchen, I spend time with him, doing what he wants to do.

Callie made a small choking sound, grabbing her water and taking a large gulp to cover her shock. The sheer, unvarnished frankness of it all was sending her bubbly personality into a system-wide crash. Seeing Callie's expression, Grace elaborated with the patience of a teacher explaining a simple concept to a struggling student. "Sometimes we play games, he likes older video games. Sometimes we'll watch a movie.

The important thing is that it's his time to decompress. I'm just there to facilitate it." She tilted her head, a glint in her eye. "Of course, atmosphere is key. When I'm in his apartment, I make sure to wear as little as possible, but never completely naked. Usually just one of his shirts with nothing underneath." Callie's mind was reeling, trying to process the image of sweet, quiet Grace executing a multi-pronged seduction campaign with the precision of a military general.

"You have to understand," Grace continued, her voice soft but firm, like velvet draped over steel. "For a man like Kyle, or a man like Junior, they carry the weight of their decisions on their shoulders all day. They are protectors, warriors. When they come back to their private space, they need to feel like they are in their own kingdom, where every need is anticipated and met. Walking that tempting thin line of seduction, being both a comforting presence and an object of desire, it makes him feel like an emperor in his own home. It's a power I give him, and in return, he gives me his love and devotion."

Callie fanned her face with her hand, the heat suddenly feeling like 110. An emperor. She tried to picture Junior, his perpetually serious expression, the way his muscles moved under his shirt when he was cleaning a rifle, as an emperor. She then tried to picture herself as the sultry, comforting empress facilitating his decompression and nearly coughed

156

water out of her nose. She'd be more likely to trip over a power cord and set the mood with a string of creative curse words than glide around in just his shirt.

"So… you do all that," Callie began, choosing her words carefully as if navigating a minefield. "You create the atmosphere, you wear the shirt, you become this… this comforting object of desire… and then?" She leaned forward, expectantly. Another small smile touched Grace's lips. It transformed her face, making her look her age for a fleeting second. "And then I take him to bed. We make love. He falls asleep feeling safe, and wanted, and completely at peace."

"Wow," Callie breathed, a slow grin spreading across her face. "Grace, you're a genius. A terrifying, Machiavellian genius. I need to take notes. This is a better project plan than half the ones I've written." Grace's smile faltered slightly, replaced by a flicker of something else, wistfulness, maybe a touch of frustration. "It's not perfect," she admitted, looking down at her hands clasped in her lap. "After he's asleep… I have to leave."

Callie blinked. "Leave? Leave and do what?" "Go back to my room. There, in the main house." Grace gestured vaguely toward the building behind them. "I can't stay the night in his apartment. It's one of David's rules. We're not officially married yet, so we don't officially cohabitate. Seth and I still have our rooms in the house with Mom."

Callie's mind screeched to a halt. All that work, all that masterful seduction and emperor-making, only to have to sneak out like a thief in the night? "You're kidding me," she said, her voice laced with indignation on Grace's behalf. "You

157

go to all that trouble to build him a kingdom for the evening, and then you get evicted from the palace at midnight?"

Grace shrugged, a small, resigned motion. "It's the way things are, for now. David is… particular. He believes in structure. Kyle and I both understand and respect it. But," she sighed, a soft puff of air in the quiet night, "I wish I could wake up with him. But…" Her eyes lighting up again, "I do bring him breakfast in the morning, and make him coffee."

Suddenly, all the disparate parts of Callie's world clicked together with the satisfying thud of a well-laid plan. The Smithy. Junior's apartment renovation. The Barn annex. Her projects. They weren't just about dirt and concrete and schedules anymore. They were about this. A new wave of purpose washed over her. Her job had just been upgraded from 'Project Manager' to 'Architect of Domestic Bliss.'

"Okay, so that's the hold-up," Callie said, her mind already shifting into problem-solving mode. "The rule. So, when does the rule… expire? When do you get to live with him full-time and not have to do the midnight walk of shame back to your dad's house?" Grace smiled softly at Callie's phrasing. "When we're married," she stated, as if it were the simplest, most obvious fact in the world.

Callie nodded, processing. "Right. Married. Of course." She did the quick math that any nineteen-year-old would do. Grace was fifteen. The normal age to get married was at least eighteen, at least. Her internal project timeline began to unspool. Eighteen minus fifteen was three. Three years. "Wow, Grace," she breathed, a genuine note of sympathy in her voice. "That's… that's a long time. Three more years of this?" The thought of a three-year project just to get two people into the same apartment full-time seemed both epic and agonizing. She could build a whole new bunker in that time.

Grace's brow furrowed in confusion, but then a look of understanding dawned on her face. She let out a small, airy laugh. "Oh, no. Not three years. Gosh, I don't think I could wait that long." She shook her head, a wistful look in her eyes. Callie's mental flowchart hit a 404 error. The data wasn't computing. "Wait, what? I thought... I mean, you're fifteen. Don't you have to be eighteen?" She felt a pang of secondhand embarrassment.

"Oh, that was an old-world thing, mostly," Grace explained patiently. "Here, David's rule is that you have to be an adult. And for the girls in the family, that's sixteen." She said it with a casual certainty. Callie stared. "Sixteen?" she repeated, the word feeling foreign and strange. "As in... one-six? The number after fifteen? So... next year?" The timeline for 'Project: Grace & Kyle's Domestic Bliss' just had its deadline slashed by two-thirds. It was dizzyingly efficient. It was also, from her pre-apocalypse perspective, completely wild. Her mind briefly flashed to old high school health classes and daytime TV dramas. This would have sent her guidance counselor into a tailspin.

"My birthday is in March," Grace added, a blush creeping onto her cheeks. "So, less than a year, really." Callie let out a low whistle, shaking her head in disbelief. "Okay. Wow. New timeline." She mentally archived the old one. "But that still leaves... nine months of you having to leave Kyle's apartment every night. Which brings me back to my original risk assessment." She leaned in again. "What would actually happen if you just... didn't? If you stayed the night? I mean, really. Would Junior get dispatched to drag you out by your ear? What's the actual penalty here?" She saw it as a simple cost-benefit analysis. Was the punishment worth circumventing for a night of uninterrupted coupledom?

Grace paused, the sudden silence amplifying the crickets. She looked at Callie, not with annoyance, but with a deep, thoughtful sincerity. "I wouldn't get in trouble," she said quietly. Callie blinked. "You wouldn't? Then what's the point..." "It's not about getting in trouble," Grace interrupted gently, her gaze unwavering. "It's about respect."

"Dad trusts me," Grace elaborated. "He trusts me because I respect him. He doesn't have to waste time or energy worrying if I'm going to do something stupid, because he knows I won't. That's the deal." She shifted. "He has... a lot to think about. My part in that is to be reliable. To not be another problem he has to solve."

"So, it's not a rule, it's a... protocol," Callie finally translated, snapping her fingers as she found a term that fit into her mental framework. "A protocol based on maintaining the operational integrity of the Patriarch. You not causing trouble lowers his cognitive load, which frees up processing power for bigger threats." She nodded, satisfied. "Okay. I get it. It's a passive support role. You're being a good team member by... not being a line item in his daily stress report."

Grace offered a small, appreciative smile. Leave it to Callie to turn a matter of the heart and filial duty into project management jargon. "Something like that, yes. But David isn't just the Patriarch, he's my father, and I want him to be proud of me." "Right then," Callie chirped, her bubbly energy returning full force.

They walked in comfortable silence for a moment, leaving the soft glow of the generator powered lights behind them. Above them, the sky was an obscene blanket of stars, unobscured by the light pollution of a dead world. "So, this Smithy," Grace began, her voice soft. "Is burying it going to be difficult?"

Callie's face lit up, her mind instantly shifting to her primary project. "Difficult? Nah. Just labor-intensive. We've got the backhoe. The main challenge is personnel. We need to move a lot of dirt, and we need spotters every step of the way." "The hardest part will be the heat," Grace noted, her own practical nature surfacing. "Even with the night shift, it's still nearly ninety degrees. We'll need a lot of water on-site."

"Already in the project plan!" Callie beamed, pointing at Grace as if she'd just scored bonus points in a game show. "Hydration logistics. Kathy's coordinating it. See? Teamwork makes the dream work." As they walked, the crunch of gravel under their boots the only sound, Callie looked off into the dark expanse beyond the ranch's perimeter. "Plus with all the noise the backhoe makes, we still have to maintain security. Out here, we don't get a lot of visitors, but we do get some, and most of them aren't friendly."

Grace nodded. "That's Junior's territory. He'll have the perimeter locked down." Callie's smile softened at the mention of his name. "Yeah. He does. Still, it's on my project risk assessment." She gave a little sigh, shifting gears again. "Speaking of teamwork, I want to go check on the crew clearing out Apartment 15 for Junior's renovation. Make sure they're not just taking sledgehammers to the place." "You're going down to the bunker now?" Grace asked. "Yep. Wanna come?" Callie's invitation was bright and genuine. "It's air-conditioned."

That was all the convincing Grace needed. "Lead the way." Their path took them to the massive work shed. To the side, a set of wide, concrete stairs descended into the earth. As they descended, the oppressive heat of the Texas night gave way to the cool air of subterranean bliss. They emerged into the long corridor, finding Apartment 15 at the far end of the hall. The door was propped open, and the sounds of grunting and scraping echoed out. Inside, the small apartment, the furniture was gone, and Andrew was currently wrestling with the refrigerator, trying to maneuver it onto a heavy-duty dolly. Susan stood by with a bottle of water, offering encouragement, while Darrel leaned against a doorframe, watching the proceedings with an air of detached amusement.

"You got it, honey," Susan said, patting his sweaty shoulder. "You'd think you were single-handedly wrestling a Decepticon, the way you're carrying on," Darrel quipped, not moving a muscle to help. "It's a machine that makes things cold, Andrew. Not a final boss." "Evening, crew!" Callie announced cheerfully as she and Grace stepped inside.

Andrew straightened up. "Callie. Thank God. Can you put a better cart on the project plan? Maybe a small crane? My vertebrae are turning to dust." Callie laughed. "Nice try. That's why there are three of you. But I'm glad you brought up the hard parts, because that's why I'm here." She glanced around the place. "Listen up, this is important. Once you start tearing down the walls and counters for Junior's new layout, I need you to disassemble, not demolish."

Andrew frowned. "Disassemble? It'd be a hell of a lot faster to just smash it out with a crowbar." "Faster, yes. Smarter, no," Callie countered, her tone still light but firm. "I want to be able to reuse as much as possible. Every cabinet door, every hinge, every sheet of drywall that we can salvage is one less thing we have to fabricate from scratch or scavenge from a rotting house fifty miles away. Think of it as a deconstruction project, not a rage room."

Darrel raised his glass in a mock toast. "See, Andrew? It's not about brute force. It's about finesse. And free labor." He winked at Callie, who just rolled her eyes good-naturedly. "Exactly," Callie said, beaming at Grace. "Resource management, people. It's what separates us from disorganized cannibals." She made a few notes on her clipboard. "Alright, now that you have your marching orders, Grace and I are going to check on the ladies next door. Keep up the… gentle work."

"You're good at that," Grace said softly, her voice barely echoing in the tunnel-like space. "Getting them to listen without yelling." Callie flashed her a grateful smile. "It's all about the cheerful, non-negotiable tone. Make it sound like the best, most logical idea they've ever heard. Now, let's see if it works on Junior's ladies." They arrived at Apartment 13. Callie gave a series of three sharp, friendly knocks. The door swung open a moment later, and her pre-planned, professional greeting, died on her lips.

Standing there was Emma, Junior's smallest wife, a warm, welcoming smile on her face. And that was far from the most noticeable thing about her. She was wearing her eternity collar. Below that, a loose, thin, white tank top hung precariously off one shoulder, the fabric doing very little to conceal the fact that she wore nothing underneath it. Completing the ensemble was a simple, elegant pair of black lace panties. And absolutely nothing else.

Callie's brain, a moment ago a machine of timelines and logistics, sputtered and system-crashed. "Callie! Grace! Come on in," Emma said, her voice as warm and breezy as her attire. She stepped aside, completely oblivious, or perhaps entirely accustomed, to the effect she was having.

Grace offered a small, shy smile and slipped past, her eyes taking in the scene. Callie, however, remained rooted to the spot for a half-second too long before her legs remembered how to function. She stepped inside, her cheeks burning.

The apartment was in a state of disorganized chaos. There were no sealed boxes or packing tape. Instead, stacks of clothing, books, and personal effects were neatly piled, ready to be carried across the hall to their temporary accommodation. It was a move in its most literal, short-distance sense.

Before Callie could formulate a sentence that didn't involve squeaking, a new presence was in her personal space. Riley, all sharp, sarcastic wit and confident grace, emerged from the bedroom. "Project Manager Barbie, here to crack the whip?" Riley purred. And then, without another word, she leaned in, cupped Callie's face in her hands, and pressed her lips to hers. It was a full, confident, and deep kiss that tasted of cinnamon and sheer audacity.

Callie's mind, which had just begun to reboot, went blue screen of death. Her tablet slipped from her numb fingers, clattering onto the floor. Her entire being was focused on the shocking, surprisingly pleasant sensation. Just as quickly as it started, Riley pulled back, a smug little smirk playing on her lips. She licked her own lips thoughtfully. "Hmm," she declared. "You taste good."

Callie stood there, blinking, her face the color of a ripe tomato. She knew, intellectually, that Junior's wives were a close-knit, affectionate unit, famously comfortable in their domestic life. David often proudly spoke of the harmony Junior had cultivated. But knowing about it and having it demonstrated via a tongue-lashing from a woman wearing yoga shorts and a sports bra were two vastly different realities.

While Callie was having her internal meltdown, Emma had already taken Grace under her wing. "Do you want something to drink, sweetie? We have water and... well, mostly water, but it's good water!" she said, guiding Grace toward the kitchenette.

Several minutes later, Callie stood there, tablet clutched to her chest like a shield, watching this incredible display of female solidarity. They weren't treating Grace like a child playing house; they were treating her as an equal, a peer. It was a beautiful thing to witness.

She took a deep breath, marshaled her scattered thoughts, and marched over to Emma, who was chatting casually with Grace about preferred kitchen utensils. Callie lowered her voice, trying to keep the frantic edge out of it. "Emma," she whispered, her voice cracking slightly. "A little help?" Emma turned, her expression one of pure, unadulterated kindness. "What's up, Cal?"

"What's up?" Callie squeaked, then forced her voice down again. "Riley. She... her mouth... my mouth... why?" Emma's smile didn't falter. If anything, it became a bit more knowing. She glanced over at Riley, who was now engaged in an animated, hands-on demonstration of a self-defense move with Olivia. "Oh, that," Emma said. "You can thank Jennifer for that."

Callie blinked. "Jennifer? David's wife, Jennifer? What does she have to do with... with that?" She gestured vaguely between herself and Riley. "Well," Emma began, her voice dropping to a soft, explanatory hum. "Riley has been spending a lot of time with her lately, helping with the garden. And Jennifer has... theories. She's been David's wife for a long time, and she believes that the key to a happy multi-partner marriage, like ours or her own, is to eliminate jealousy at its root." Callie was still lost. "Okay... and the root of jealousy is... kissing the project manager?"

A light, musical laugh escaped Emma. "No, silly. The root is insecurity and competition. Jennifer's philosophy is that co-wives get along better, like, truly, deeply better, if they share intimacy. Not just emotional support, but physical affection. Hugs, cuddles, even kisses. It builds a bond that's separate from the husband. It turns you from rivals into a team. A unit."

Emma paused, letting the revolutionary concept sink into Callie's brain. "Riley," she continued, "is nothing if not dedicated. She adores Junior, and she wants our family unit to be as strong as David's. She sees how well it works for Jennifer and Jessica and the others. They're practically inseparable."

A horrifying, supernova-bright flash of understanding exploded in Callie's brain. She looked from Emma's earnest face to Riley, who was now laughing. It wasn't random. It wasn't a power play. It was... proactive team-building. "So," Callie said slowly, her voice flat with dawning realization. "She kissed me... because she thinks I'm...?" Emma's smile was bright and final. "Don't kid yourself Cal. We know why you took this project on. And don't think Junior hasn't noticed either. It's not a matter of if, it's a matter of when."

Then the door opened. "How's the move coming along?" Junior asked, his voice a low rumble that did funny things to Callie's insides. "You all doing okay? Need me to lift anything heavy?" He asked as he stepped fully inside, the door swinging shut behind him with a solid, definitive thud.

The moment that sound echoed through the apartment, a switch flipped in Emma. With a blissful sigh, her hands went to the hem of her tank top, and she began to peel it off, taking a deliberate step towards him. "You're finally here," she murmured, her eyes locked on his.

Callie's jaw tightened. They were... they were just going to... right here? With the stuff laid out? And Grace? And... her? Before Emma's hands made it to the hem of her underwear, Olivia moved quickly, placing a gentle but firm hand on Emma's arm. "Emma, honey. Not right now." Emma paused, looking at Olivia with a flicker of confusion, like a puppy who'd been told it couldn't have the treat it was just offered. "But he's home."

Olivia tilted her head pointedly towards the corner of the room where Grace was standing, seemingly oblivious. "Junior's sister is still here," Olivia whispered, her voice a model of patient correction. A little 'oh' of understanding formed on Emma's lips. She straightened up, grabbing her top from the floor with a slight, theatrical pout, but there was no real frustration in it.

"Looks like you're making good progress," he said. He looked past them, his gaze softening as it landed on his sister. "Hey, Gracie. Thanks for helping them out." Grace offered a shy, sweet smile. "It's no problem, Junior. Callie's really good at telling everyone what to do." Callie felt a little jolt of pride at the compliment, managing a professional smile.

Junior's attention snapped to her, closing the distance between them in two long steps. The sheer force of his sudden presence was overwhelming. "Callie," he said, his voice dropping even lower. And then, before she took her next breath, his hand was on the small of her back, warm and firm through the thin fabric of her shirt. He pulled her flush against him. The tablet slipped from her numb fingers, clattering to the floor, again. The world narrowed to the scent of him, the solid wall of his chest, and the intense look in his eyes, as he leaned in and kissed her.

Callie's mind, body, and soul felt like a goddamn supernova. Her brain, gone. A whirlwind of lustful longing, so potent and so sudden, ripped through her, making her toes curl in her boots. It tasted of coffee and confidence, and it felt like every fantasy she'd ever had about him was being mainlined directly into her central nervous system. She felt herself melt into him, her hands coming up to grip his shoulders as if it were the only thing keeping her anchored to the planet.

Just as quickly as it began, it was over. Junior pulled back, leaving her swaying slightly, her lips tingling, her entire body humming like a live wire. He bent down, picked up her tablet, and placed it back in her hands. "I appreciate the work you're doing. I'm proud of you." Callie could only stare at him. She tried to form a word. "Uh," she managed. He gave her a final, appraising nod before turning back to his wives. "Alright, let's get the last of this moved so she can do her job."

Callie stood frozen in place, her fingers clutching the tablet so hard the paper started to crumble. She could hear the others resuming their tasks, their voices a muffled buzz in the background. Her own internal monologue, however, was screaming. Her heart was trying to beat its way out of her ribcage, a frantic drum against the sudden, shocking warmth that had pooled low in her belly. Her brain felt like a bag of spaghetti. And somewhere in that scrambled, static-filled mess, one coherent, mortifying, and undeniably true thought crystalized with stunning clarity. "Oh my god. I think I just came a little."

Chapter 22:

The Beast's Wild Harvest

"You sure about this?" Scott asked, loading a heavy-duty transport cage into the surprisingly spacious trunk. His son, Mike, shadowed him, trying to match his father's efficiency and mostly just getting in the way. "Seems like asking a thoroughbred to pull a plow." Kyle sighed, jingling the keys in his hand. "Aidan's orders. He said, and I quote, 'She's got the torque and the suspension, can handle the rough roads better than the truck.' He also threatened to weld my favorite rifle to the ceiling if I scratch her." "He wouldn't," Mike said, his eyes wide. "He would," Kyle and Scott said in unison.

A light, confident step sounded on the gravel behind them. "She'll be fine, my love," Grace said, her voice calm. She directed the words to Kyle, but her eyes swept over Scott and Mike. Kyle let out a breath. "I know, I know. It's just... it's Aidan's baby." "Aidan knows we need the piglets more than he needs to win a best build at a car show," Grace countered, stopping beside him to pat the cherry-red hood. "Besides, Aidan built this car to work, not to sit in the bunker."

Scott grunted, finally shoving the last pig cage into the trunk. The fit was snug, but luckily the trunk was wide. "Let's get this show on the road before the sun's up properly. Pigs won't wait for us to debate automotive engineering." He was happy, truly happy. The thought of raising their own pigs, of having a steady supply of pork for bacon, chops, and sausage, was a comforting vision of normalcy.

Mike, vibrating with a teenager's cocktail of excitement and nerves, clambered into the back seat. "This is so cool. It smells like oranges and... victory." Scott slid in beside his son, the dense upholstery stretching against their weapons. Kyle took the driver's seat with the reverence of a priest approaching an altar, while Grace hopped into the passenger seat, immediately propping her boots up on the dashboard.

Kyle flinched. "Grace. The dash." "It's fine," she said, not moving them. "Adds character." Kyle's hands remained perfectly still on the steering wheel. He didn't turn the key. He didn't even look at her. He just stared through the pristine windshield at the inky blackness that was slowly fading to a deep indigo. The Beast's powerful engine remained silent, a sleeping giant in the pre-dawn hush.

"Kyle," Grace said, her voice dropping the playful tone. "We're burning moonlight." "Feet on the floor, Grace," he replied, his voice low and devoid of compromise. From the back seat, Scott shifted his weight, the seat groaning in protest. "Uh, what's the hold-up? We out of propane?" "No, Dad," Mike piped up, leaning forward between the front seats. "It's a domestic dispute."

Kyle shot a look into the rearview mirror, catching Mike's grin. "It's a safety issue." He finally turned his head to look at Grace. "If I have to swerve or hit something, and that airbag goes off... Grace, your knees will go through your eye sockets. You'll be folded in half like a cheap lawn chair. I'm not letting that happen."

Grace's expression softened slightly at his genuine concern, but her stubborn streak was a mile wide. She gestured with a thumb towards the thick, black metal tubes that framed the car's interior, running along the roofline and down the A-pillars. "Kyle, look around. This isn't a normal car. It's a roll cage with wheels and paint. The entire frame is a chromoly cage. Aidan said you could drive it off a cliff and the passenger cabin would be fine. I'm safer in here with my feet up than I am walking to the barn."

"I don't care if it's forged by dwarves in the heart of a mountain," Kyle retorted, his patience fraying. The image of her mangled body was seared into his brain, a horror film he refused to let premiere. "You have two options. Feet on the floor, or you can get in the back and discuss the finer points of hog-trapping with Mike."

Grace stared him down, her jaw set. For a moment, the tension in the car was thicker than the humidity outside. Scott wisely remained silent, though Mike watched the exchange with the rapt attention of someone at a tennis match. Finally, with a theatrical sigh that could have powered a small windmill, Grace swung her legs down. Her boots hit the floor mat with a definitive thud. "Fine," she muttered, crossing her arms over the tactical vest strapped to her chest. "You're an overprotective, dashboard-obsessed tyrant." "I can live with that," Kyle said, a wave of relief washing over him as he turned the key.

The Beast purred to life, but it was a sound Mike hadn't expected. He was used to the rumble and roar of the Behemoth, or the clatter of the generator. This was different. Aidan's creation idled with a low, almost gentle purr, a deep thrum that vibrated through the floor mats but barely disturbed the pre-dawn quiet. Mike glanced at the custom dashboard, a glowing array of analog gauges that looked like something out of a racing circuit. He was genuinely surprised; a car that looked this aggressive should have woken half the county. It was like a panther, all coiled muscle and silent potential.

As Kyle skillfully navigated the Beast off the ranch's gravel drive and onto the cracked asphalt of the old county road, the quietude vanished. He eased onto what was once a two-lane highway, now a graveyard of skeletal, rust-eaten vehicles. Finding a clear stretch, he looked in the rearview mirror, met Scott's eyes, and gave a slight nod. Then he pressed the accelerator.

The reaction was instantaneous. A high-pitched whine, like a jet engine spooling up, screamed from under the hood as the dual turbos force-fed air into the Boxer engine. The quiet hum erupted into a ferocious snarl, and all four occupants were unceremoniously slammed back into their racing seats. Mike's stomach lurched into his throat, his wide eyes glued to the speedometer as the dials whipped clockwise. Outside, the derelict cars became a continuous, rusted streak. Grace, despite her earlier protests, let out an involuntary "Whoa!" Her hands, which had been crossed stubbornly over her chest, shot out to grip the integrated handle on the door.

The sheer, brutal force of the acceleration was a physical argument that dwarfed any of her verbal ones.

Kyle eased off the gas, and the Beast settled into a powerful, ground-eating cruise. The G-force subsided, allowing everyone to breathe again. The turbo's whine faded back into the deep, resonant purr of the engine. In the back seat, Scott adjusted his seatbelt, a look of pure, unadulterated shock and delight on his face. He leaned forward, his voice filled with the awe of a man who appreciated fine machinery. "Holy hell, Kyle," he breathed, his voice a little hoarse. "Did Aidan really... build this himself? I mean, from scratch?"

Kyle chuckled, but kept his eyes on the road. "God's honest truth, Scott. Every nut and bolt. Though it didn't always look... or sound... like this." He glanced in the rearview again, a nostalgic glint in his eyes. "You know, when I first met him, almost eleven years ago now, my older brother Jason and I were damn sure this thing was a death trap waiting to happen. We were... skeptical, to put it mildly."

He navigated a particularly nasty stretch of debris before continuing. "David hadn't moved the whole family to Texas yet. He was still based in Arizona, and he'd rented the house right next door to his for us. The whole reason we were there was so Jason and I could train Junior, get him started on the path to being a master gunsmith like he is now. And while we were in the garage all day, swapping out trigger assemblies and lapping barrels, Aidan was in his garage."

Kyle laughed again, a fuller sound this time. "He was fifteen, Scott, fifteen years old. And he was out there welding together what looked like a Frankenstein's monster on

175

wheels. The body was mostly scrap metal he'd scrounged. I think the original chassis was from a wrecked Subaru, but that was a few years before we ever saw it. Eventually he had a Chromoly ladder-body chassis built. He was telling anyone who would listen that he was building a propane-powered car. Jason and I used to bet on which day it would either fall apart or explode. Never did."

In the back seat, Mike shifted his weight. His eyes were wide with a mix of awe and disbelief. "Wait a minute," he said, his voice cracking slightly with adolescent enthusiasm. "You said the first chassis was from a few years before you saw it. He must have started building this thing when he was, like, twelve?"

Mike leaned forward. "So, how old were you, then?" Before Kyle could answer, Grace piped up, her voice clear and certain. "He was twenty-one." She said. "I remember it." Scott leaned forward. "You remember that? You couldn't have been more than a pipsqueak." "I was four," Grace stated. "It was a big deal. Aunt Kayla, Kyle's sister, had been part of the family for a few years at that point, and that was also when Aidan met Alissa."

The casual way she recounted events from her own childhood was still a trip for the uninitiated. Mike, however, was used to it. He processed the information, his mind buzzing. "Okay, so you're twenty-one, a total stranger to the family except for your sister. And there's this four-year-old girl running around, who you barely even notice." He paused, a mischievous look in his eyes as he looked directly at Kyle.

"What would you have said back then if someone told you that in eleven years, you'd be engaged to that pipsqueak?"

Kyle, who had been taking a sip from his canteen, promptly choked. He sputtered, water dribbling down his chin as a coughing fit seized him. Scott roared with laughter, slapping his knee. "Oh, that's a good one, Mike! Ask the real questions!" Grace calmly reached over and patted Kyle's back, her touch gentle but firm. "Breathe, Kyle. It's a hypothetical question, not a death sentence."

Wiping his mouth with the back of his hand, Kyle shot a glare at the rearview mirror, his face flushed. "Thanks, Mike. Really appreciate you trying to give me an aneurysm before sunrise." "C'mon!" Scott goaded, still chuckling. "Spit it out, lover boy. What would twenty-one-year-old you have done? Probably run for the hills, I bet." Kyle didn't answer and just kept driving, occasionally glancing at Grace.

Scott just egged him on. "Quit stallin', Romeo. The boy asked a question. Picture it: you're twenty-one, probably chasing tail in Tucson, thinkin' you're hot stuff. Some weirdo comes up and says, 'Hey, see that little four-year-old over there picking her nose? That's your future wife.' What's your play?" "It was pollen, and I had a tissue," Grace said. "And for the record, Kyle wasn't 'hot stuff.' He was mostly just broke."

Kyle groaned, dropping his head against the steering wheel for a second. "Okay! Fine! You want to know? I would have laughed in their face. Then I would have checked to see if they were on something. Then I probably would have called the cops, in this hypothetical scenario where someone from the future is giving me unsolicited dating advice about a toddler."

He lifted his head, a resigned sigh escaping his lips. "I was a twenty-one-year-old gunsmith, fresh out of school. My entire world revolved around finding a clean pair of socks, affording cheap beer, and figuring out how to pay my rent. The idea of settling down, let alone with a literal child I barely knew existed, would have been so far off my radar, it wouldn't even be in the same solar system. I would have dismissed it as the ramblings of a lunatic."

Mike nodded thoughtfully, processing this. "That's fair." "No, no, not fair yet," Scott interjected, his eyes gleaming with mischief. He leaned forward, propping his elbows on the back of Kyle's seat, his voice dropping conspiratorially. "So after David moved to Texas, you just went back to Tucson and lived like a monk for two and a half years? Waiting for a grade-schooler three states over?"

Kyle's hands tightened on the wheel. He shot a quick glance at Grace, who seemed utterly unfazed, her attention fixed on scanning the horizon. "No, Scott. I didn't live like a monk." He braced himself. "I had a girlfriend." Mike's eyebrows shot up. Scott leaned back with a triumphant, breathy, "Aha! The plot thickens! Details, man, details! What was she like? A librarian? A schoolteacher? Please tell me she was young and impressionable."

Before Kyle could formulate a defense for a life that felt like it belonged to another person, Grace's calm, even voice cut through the cabin, not even turning her head. "Her name was Allie. With an 'i'. She was a welder. Twenty-eight, so a bit older. Lots of tattoos, a whole sleeve of what looked like angry koi fish on her left arm. Very insecure." The interior of the Beast fell silent, save for the engine's thrum. Kyle, Scott, and Mike all turned their heads toward Grace. "How in the world," Kyle finally managed, his voice a choked whisper, "do you know all of that?"

Grace finally turned, her observant eyes meeting his. "Kayla used to call you a lot, trying to convince you to move out here. I could usually tell what you two were talking about, by reading her lips." Kyle let out a breath that sounded suspiciously like a deflating tire. The surprise was gone, replaced by a familiar sense of profound, almost weary resignation. Of course. Of course, Grace knew.

He shook his head, a small, wry smile touching his lips. He glanced at Mike in the rearview mirror. The boy looked utterly spooked, as if Grace had just revealed she could levitate. "Lesson for the day, Mike," Kyle said, his voice regaining its equilibrium. "Never, and I mean never, assume you have a secret if Grace is in the same time zone. The girl has… talents. Lip-reading is the least surprising of them."

Scott let out a cackle that filled the car, slapping his knee. "Oh, this is better than HBO! So not only is our pint-sized vanguard a walking tactical computer, she's also a one-woman TMZ. This is fantastic!" He leaned forward again, the mischief back in his eyes full-force. "Okay, okay, don't get sidetracked. We've established the how. Now, back to the why. A welder with an angry koi fish tattoo. So, you dumped her because her body art was too aggressive?"

"No, Scott," Kyle sighed. "Was it the insecurity? Did she cry every time you complimented another woman's welds?" Scott pressed, rubbing his hands together. "C'mon, man. We've got a long drive. Entertain us." "It wasn't that simple," Kyle grumbled, knowing it was a losing battle. "Look, part of it was practical. Tucson was getting oversaturated. Too many guys doing what I do, not enough work to go around. Kayla had been telling me for a year that David needed a dedicated gunsmith out here, that the family was growing and the armory needed a full-time manager. Business was drying up. That was the logical part."

"Ah, the 'logical' part," Scott said, drawing out the word. "Which means it's the boring cover story for the real, juicy part. Let's have it." Kyle shot another glance at Grace. She was looking out the window again. She knew the rest of the story. He might as well just tell it. "Allie had an ex," he said, his tone flat. "A real piece of work. The kind of guy who thought child support was a suggestion and that his name on the birth certificate gave him permanent squatting rights in her life. He'd show up at all hours, drunk or high, screaming about how she 'owed him' and how I was trying to steal his family."

Mike winced. "That's rough." "It was a headache," Kyle corrected. "She was a good person, mostly, but she couldn't cut him loose. I'd come over and he'd be passed out on her couch. I offered to help her get a restraining order, offered to pay the filing fees. I even changed her locks for her twice. The last straw was when he showed up at my shop, started mouthing off to my last few customers, and tried to pick a fight. That kind of liability is… bad for business. Bad for life."

The cabin was quiet again, Scott's jokey demeanor momentarily deflated. Then, Grace's voice, soft but clear, cut through the engine's hum. "He wasn't worth the trouble. And she didn't deserve you." All three men looked at her. She didn't turn this time, her focus entirely on the mission. "I heard you talking to Aunt Kayla about it. You thought she deserved better, but she still expected you to pay for her mistakes. You were too kind," Grace stated, as if it were a simple, observable fact. "She wasn't. She was irresponsible and a manipulator."

"So, Kyle, my man," Scott began, his tone shifting back into one of pure, unadulterated mischief. "I gotta ask. Be honest with your old pal Scott. Is it… frustrating?" He gestured with a thumb towards Grace. "Having a fiancée who's basically got a mental cheat sheet to your entire past? No skeletons in your closet because she's already cataloged them, laminated the file, and knows precisely which ones will rattle the loudest if she jiggles the handle."

Mike turned his head to look at Kyle, his young face a mask of genuine curiosity. Kyle kept his eyes on the broken white line of the road ahead, navigating the car around a rusted-out sedan. He let the question sit for a second before answering, giving it the consideration it deserved. "Nah," he finally said, his voice even. "It's only frustrating if she uses that knowledge for evil." "For evil?" Mike piped up, his voice cracking slightly. "Like what?"

"Oh, you know," Kyle said, glancing in the rearview mirror, then his eyes briefly met Grace's before flicking back to the road. "Like the constant, soul-crushing 'I told you so' every time you make a mistake, she already saw you make ten years ago. Or the preemptive strike: 'I know what you're thinking, so don't even think about it.' Holding every past misstep over your head like some kind of relationship blackmail."

He expertly swerved the Beast off the pavement and onto a dirt track. "But Grace has never done that. Not once," he continued, his tone softening with an undeniable undercurrent of affection. "She's never criticized me for a mistake I made, technically. She's never once tried to control me or box me in based on something she knows. Honestly, she's never even brought something up unless somebody else does first, like I just did. If I mess up, she's there to help me fix it, not to tell me she knew I would."

He paused, navigating a particularly nasty rut. "It's actually the opposite of frustrating. It's... peaceful. It's like having a partner who gets the whole story, not just the current chapter, and still chooses to be there. She doesn't have to guess why I'm quiet sometimes or why I get a certain look on my face when I'm dealing with something difficult. She just... knows. And she lets it be."

The cabin fell quiet again, but this time it was a comfortable, thoughtful silence. Then, Grace finally turned from the window. "It's not about knowing secrets," she said, her voice clear and steady over the engine's hum. "It's about knowing him. All that stuff from before, the ex-girlfriend, the business struggles, even the problems he faces now... it's all data. It helps me understand the man he is now. Why he's so patient. Why he's protective. Why he values honesty so much." She looked directly at Kyle, and for a second, the age difference between them seemed to evaporate, replaced by a connection that was profound and absolute.

"He's allowed to have his own thoughts," Grace stated, turning her calm gaze to Scott and Mike. "His own space. His own secrets, if he wants them. I don't need to live inside his head. I just need to be by his side. It's not my job to police his past or his future. My job is to love the man he's become because of all of it." She gave a small, almost imperceptible smile. "Trying to control someone isn't love; it's management. My dad manages the ranch, but I'm going to marry my husband."

Mike just stared. "Whoa," he breathed. Scott blinked slowly, his jokey facade completely dismantled by the sheer weight of her wisdom. He was speechless for a solid five seconds before he recovered, slapping a hand on his son's knee. "See, Mike?" Scott said, his voice regaining its familiar, teasing cadence. "That's what you look for in a woman. Not just the one that's pretty, but the one who's smart enough to know your baggage makes you interesting and who will let you have your secrets. Like where you hide that extra slice of Jennifer's pecan pie." "Dad, oh my god," Mike groaned, burying his face in his hands as Kyle and Scott chuckled.

Back at the ranch, the air in the Smithy was thick with the smell of fresh-cut pine, damp earth, and hard work. The building was a cavern of cool concrete and shadows. Josh was wiping sweat from his brow with the back of a gloved hand, admiring his handiwork. He'd constructed a sturdy double-gate system at the main entrance, a smaller gate set within a larger one, designed for people to slip through without giving a panicked piglet an escape route.

"Solid as a rock," he declared with a satisfied country drawl, giving the heavy wooden frame a final, solid shake. "A Brahman bull couldn't get through that." Inside, Lily was wrestling a heavy, prefabricated stall panel into place, her muscles flexing under her tank top. She grunted with effort, securing it to a post Josh had set earlier. "A Brahman bull isn't what we're trying to keep in here, genius," she shot back, a playful smirk on her face. "We're containing a half-dozen squealing, mud-loving hellions. They're smarter than a bull."

"And you're smarter than them," Josh said, walking over to help her with the next panel. He leaned in and kissed her cheek. "And prettier, too." Lily scoffed, pushing a stray strand of hair from her face. "Flattery will get you everywhere, farm boy. Now grab the other end of this before I decide to use it to pin you to the wall."

Just then, the heavy door to the Smithy creaked open, spilling a stripe of golden morning light across the dusty floor. Tiffany and Nicole entered, their arms laden with supplies. Tiffany carried a roll of heavy-duty hose and a box of industrial cleaning supplies. Nicole, her sweet nature evident in her careful handling of the items, carried two large buckets and a stack of fresh towels. "Looks like you two are making good progress," Tiffany said, her voice echoing slightly in the large space. She set her load down with a purposeful thud. "David would be pleased."

Nicole smiled warmly, placing her buckets next to Tiffany's supplies. "It's going to be perfect for them. We need to make sure the drainage is clear before we lay down the first layer of straw. We want them to be as comfortable as possible during their quarantine." Josh grinned. "You talkin' about the pigs or me and Lily? 'Cause we'd like to be comfortable too."

Lily rolled her eyes, heaving another panel into alignment. "Ignore him. His brain melts a little when it's hot." "It's all part of my country charm, darlin'," he retorted, moving behind her to 'help' brace the panel. His hands found her waist, his body pressing lightly against her back. "Just gotta hold it steady."

Lily could feel the heat radiating from him, mingling with her own. The air was already warm, and their work had made it feel ten degrees hotter. She could feel a trickle of sweat run down the valley of her back. "Okay, okay, it's set, you can let go now," she said, trying to wiggle out of his grasp. "Josh, stop. I'm disgusting and all sweaty."

Instead of letting go, Josh's grip on Lily's waist tightened just enough to be possessive. He leaned in, his breath warm against her skin. "Don't care," he murmured, his voice a low, rumbling vibration against her back. Before she could protest again, he licked her, his tongue tracing a slow, deliberate path from the sensitive curve of her neck up to the shell of her ear. A shiver, completely involuntary and entirely unrelated to the heat, shot down Lily's spine.

She gasped, her hands flying up to shove at his chest, though there was no real force behind it. "Josh! Ugh, you're impossible!" she sputtered, her cheeks flushing a deep red. She managed to twist out of his grasp, putting a few feet of dusty air between them, her eyes wide with a mixture of exasperation and undeniable pleasure. "Tiffany and Nicole are right there."

Josh, completely unabashed, wiped his mouth with the back of his hand. "Just showin' my wife some appreciation. It's hard work, makin' a pigsty." He gave Lily a wink, which earned him an eye-roll so severe it was a wonder her head didn't spin. Then, his expression shifted. The playful expression was replaced by a look of genuine thoughtfulness. He turned his attention from Lily to Tiffany. "Speakin' of quarantine," he began. "It got me thinkin'. David mentioned somethin' a while back... about how wild hogs can carry all sorts of nasty stuff. He mentioned hepatitis specifically, I think. Do we... do we have a way of actually testing them for diseases? Or are we just gonna lock 'em in here, cross our fingers, and hope for the best?"

Tiffany's smirk faded, replaced by a look of professional focus. This was her domain. She pushed off the panels and walked towards the center of the large, empty space, her boots kicking up small puffs of dust. "That's an excellent question, Josh. And you're right, David was very concerned about it," she began, her voice taking on the authoritative yet maternal tone of an expert. "Zoonotic diseases are one of the fastest ways a community like ours could be crippled. We have a multi-step protocol. First, is simple observation. When Kyle and the others bring them in, I'll do a full visual inspection. We'll be looking for lesions on the skin, jaundice in the eyes, emaciation, signs of diarrhea, neurological issues like stumbling or circling. Any pig showing obvious signs of sickness won't even make it into quarantine. It'll be dispatched and buried deep, far from our water supply."

She paused. "The ones that look healthy come in here. The minimum quarantine period will be forty-five days. That's long enough for most common swine illnesses to present themselves." "But what about the ones that don't show symptoms?" Josh pressed, leaning forward slightly. "The carriers." "That," Tiffany said, a flicker of pride in her eyes, "is where David's foresight comes in. He, Summer, and I spent months researching and stockpiling before the fall. We have a limited supply of veterinary diagnostic kits. Specifically, we have ELISA field test kits for Porcine Reproductive and Respiratory Syndrome, Pseudorabies, and, yes, a rapid antibody test for Hepatitis, which is the big one we worry about for human transmission."

Nicole listened intently, her expression one of awe. "David really did think of everything." "He did," Tiffany affirmed. "About a week into the quarantine, once they've settled, I'll sedate them one by one and draw blood. We can run the tests right here in the clinic. It's not a full-scale lab, but it's more than anyone else in a hundred-mile radius has, I guarantee you that. Any animal that tests positive is culled. No exceptions. The health of our children and our future food supply is too important." Lily let out a low whistle.

"Damn, Tiff. I knew you were the animal guru, but that's some next-level preparedness."

Josh, however, wasn't quite satisfied. He scrubbed a hand over the scruff on his jaw, his brow furrowed. He was thinking about the world as it was now. "Hold on a second, Tiff," he said, his voice earnest. "You're talking about pig diseases. That's great, and I'm glad you got it covered. But these ain't farm-raised hogs we're talking about. They've been out there for over a year. Scavenging." He paused. "They've likely been... you know. Eating things they shouldn't. People."

Nicole's expression faltered, a flicker of unease crossing her features at the grim but necessary thought. Josh pressed on, wanting to be clear. "What about people diseases? You mentioned Hepatitis, but what about Hepatitis B? Or... hell, I don't know, whatever else you can get from a corpse that's been baking in the Texas sun? Can that stuff jump to us from the pork?"

Tiffany met his gaze and gave him a slow, appraising nod. It was a gruesome question, but a smart one. A practical one. She took a breath, shifting from maternal matriarch to clinical professor in a heartbeat. "That's an excellent, if grim, question, Josh. And the answer is complex, but ultimately reassuring." She held up a finger. "First, let's differentiate. The test we have is for Hepatitis E, or HEV. That's the one primarily associated with swine and can, on rare occasions, be transmitted to humans through undercooked pork. It's our primary concern from a zoonotic standpoint. Hepatitis B, or HBV, is a human virus. While there have been a few fringe studies on experimental transmission to pigs in a lab setting, the consensus is that they are not a natural reservoir for HBV. The virus simply doesn't thrive or replicate well in their systems. The chances of a pig contracting a viable, transmissible HBV infection from scavenging are, for all practical purposes, zero."

She took another breath, warming to her subject. "As for other theoretical pathogens from human remains… you have to remember how transmission works. Most viruses and bacteria are fragile. They require a living host. Once the host dies, they break down rapidly, especially in high heat. Prion diseases, like Kuru or CJD, are a different story, but they're exceptionally rare and primarily affect neural tissue, which the pigs would be unlikely to consume in significant amounts. Our biggest real-world threat from scavenging isn't some exotic zombie plague, it's good old-fashioned bacterial contamination, E. coli, Salmonella, Trichinosis. And our strict quarantine, cooking procedures, and Scott's meticulous butchering practices will mitigate those risks."

Tiffany snapped her fingers, a small, sharp sound that concluded her lecture with an air of finality. "And besides all that," she finished, a reassuring smile gracing her lips, "everyone here was vaccinated against Hepatitis A and B years ago as a precaution. We also have more field test kits for bacterial loads than we know what to do with, thanks to David's foresight. We'll be fine." Josh blinked slowly. His brain seemed to be buffering Tiffany's torrent of information on zoonotic pathogens, viral fragility, and prion diseases. He just wanted to know if the bacon was going to be weird. He finally managed a weak, "Oh. Okay. Good."

Chapter 23:

The Weakest Daughter

The rumble of The Beast's engine died, leaving behind a sudden, ringing silence. In the dim pre-dawn light, the air was already thick with the heavy promise of another scorching Texas day. For a moment, no one moved. The weight of Grace's words still hung in the air, a profound statement that had completely disarmed the usual morning banter.

Kyle turned off the rest of the car's systems, the interior lights fading to black. He glanced over at Grace, his expression a mixture of profound respect and deep affection. The way she had articulated their entire relationship, not just to Scott and Mike but perhaps even to herself, left him feeling a sense of rightness that settled deep in his bones.

"Right then," Scott finally boomed, shattering the stillness. He scrubbed a hand over his face, his usual jovial mask firmly back in place. "Last one out is a rotten feral hog!" He playfully shoved Mike's shoulder, who was still looking at Grace with an expression of pure, unadulterated awe. "Dad, I'm not twelve," Mike mumbled, but his protest lacked any real heat.

The four of them spilled out of the car, the sudden Texas heat hitting them like a physical blow. Scott and Mike shouldered their AR-15s as they moved. Kyle did the same, his eyes scanning the perimeter out of habit. Grace, however, moved with a different kind of purpose. Her gaze wasn't on the horizon, but on the ground. She ignored the banter, her mind already on the task ahead. Crouching low, she moved with a fluid, stealthy grace, her eyes tracing patterns in the dirt that were invisible to the others. She pointed a finger at a series of scuffs and cloven hoof prints.

"They were here less than an hour ago," she said, her voice a low murmur. "A whole sounder. See the drag marks? Piglets. They're sticking close to a water source and their bedding grounds." She moved forward, weaving through the scrubby mesquite and live oaks, her P365 snug in its thigh holster, her rifle held at a low ready. Kyle, Scott, and Mike fell into a protective diamond formation around her, their own roles as guards secondary to hers as the tracker.

"She's like a little bloodhound, ain't she?" Scott whispered to Kyle, a genuine note of admiration in his voice. "Tiffany taught her some of that, but the rest... that's David's kid, through and through." Kyle just nodded, a proud smile touching his lips. Grace stopped abruptly near a dense thicket of yaupon holly. "This is it," she announced, her voice firm. "This is a major thoroughfare for them. We'll build the trap here. A funnel." She turned to face them, her expression all business. The sweet girl from the car was gone, replaced by a field commander. "We need poles. Lots of them. Cut branches from these trees, at least an inch thick. Strip them clean. No leaves, no small twigs."

The three men looked at one another. Scott, ever the pragmatist, hitched his rifle onto his back. "Alright, boss. How many we talkin'?" Grace met his gaze without blinking, her expression unreadable. "Until I say stop." A collective groan, half-joking, half-sincere, went through the men. "You hear that, Mike?" Scott clapped his son on the back. "The lady wants poles. Let's get to work before she decides we're not pulling our weight and trades us for a couple of good goats."

"Dad!" Mike groaned, his face flushing, but he quickly pulled out a sturdy combat knife and got to work on a low-hanging mesquite branch. The next hour was a symphony of hacking, sawing, and scraping. Kyle, ever the prepared survivor, used a folding saw from his pack, his movements precise and economical. He'd cut a thick branch, strip it with swift, clean strokes of his knife, and add it to the growing pile before moving to the next.

Scott, more brute force than finesse, used a small hatchet, the rhythmic thwack-thwack-thwack echoing in the quiet morning. Mike worked with a fierce, determined energy, trying to keep up with the older men. He'd occasionally glance at Grace, who was filling sandbags and inspecting their work, testing the strength of a pole or pointing out a branch that wasn't stripped cleanly enough. He desperately wanted her approval. "Look at him go," Scott stage-whispered to Kyle, nodding towards his son. "Trying to win your fiancée's favor with a perfectly denuded branch. A true modern romance." Kyle chuckled softly. "Let him be, Scott. He's working hard."

The Texas sun, now fully clear of the horizon, began its relentless assault. The air, once cool and crisp, grew thick and heavy. A mountain of stripped pecan wood and oak poles lay in a disorderly pile, a testament to three hours of grueling, sweat-soaked labor. Scott straightened up with a groan that seemed to emanate from his very soul, pressing a hand to the small of his back. "Alright, I'm calling it," he declared to the sky. "That's at least four dozen. Maybe five. If a pig can get through a fence made of that, it deserves to be free. It can have my rifle and my spot in the bunker, the clever bastard."

"Alright," Grace announced, sliding her pack off her shoulder and setting it carefully on the ground. "Time for phase two." Scott wiped his brow with a bandana. "Phase two? I was hoping phase two involved a siesta and a cold beer. My weary bones are staging a protest." Grace ignored him, her focus entirely on the task at hand. She unbuckled a series of straps on the pack and pulled out a tightly bundled object. With a flick of her wrists, she unfurled a massive, dark green net woven from a thin, impossibly strong cord. It cascaded onto the dusty ground like a fisherman's dream. She then produced a spool of what looked like several hundred yards of 550 paracord.

Mike stared, his eyes wide. "What is that for?" "The trap," Grace said simply, as if it were the most obvious thing in the world. She sized up the pile of branches, her expression one of intense calculation. "Kyle, I need you to help me lay out the longest branches into a circle. Eighteen feet in diameter. At least two branches thick, overlap the ends."

Kyle simply nodded. "You got it." He grabbed one end of a lengthy oak branch. Scott watched, looking from the diminutive fifteen-year-old girl to the mountain of lumber. "A circle? Sweetheart, we're catching pigs, not holding a séance. My back has already communicated with the spirits, and they're telling me to sit down." "It's a corral trap," Grace corrected him without looking up, already grabbing the paracord. "A top-down drop style corral trap. We need a corral. Now, arrange the branches."

With a sigh that sounded like a deflating balloon, Scott grabbed the another oak branch. "Alright, alright, a séance it is. Mike, son, if I start speaking in tongues, just nod and tell your mother the spirits were very complimentary of her cooking." Mike, trying to suppress a grin, simply hefted a smaller branch, ready to assist. Kyle, ever the pragmatist, was already positioning a second layer of branches. He glanced at Grace, awaiting her inspection.

"bring those closer together, Scott," Grace instructed, her eyes narrowed in concentration, hands on her hips. "We need the circle to be as perfect as possible for even weight distribution." "Weight distribution," Scott grumbled, shuffling his feet and adjusting his grip on the rough bark. "Back in my day, we trapped pigs with a simple pit and some corn. Took two hours. Didn't require advanced geometry or a team of civil engineers. And my vertebrae weren't staging a class-action lawsuit against the rest of my body." He shot a look at Mike. "See? It's starting. The spirits of my ancestors are complaining through me."

Grace didn't even bother to look up from the coil of paracord in her hands. Her small fingers, surprisingly nimble and strong, were already working a knot. "You used a pit trap back in your day, Scott, because you were trying to trap a pig. I'm not trying to trap a pig." She paused, letting the statement hang in the humid morning air. She finally lifted her gaze, her eyes, sharp and intelligent, pinning him in place. "I'm trapping the whole sounder."

"It's more efficient," Grace stated flatly, turning her attention back to her work. "You separate a sow from her piglets, or a dominant boar from the group, you cause panic. Now, the circle." Kyle grunted, a sound of comprehension and approval. "Makes sense." He hefted his end of the pole. "You heard the boss, Scott." "The boss," Scott muttered, readjusting his grip. "She's getting more like David every day. All grand plans and unnerving logic. It's creepy." He shuffled into position, mirroring Kyle. "Alright, pig princess, where do you want this holy log of porcine summoning?"

Just as Scott was about to straighten up and celebrate the completion of their pagan monument, Grace pointed to a spot inside the ring. "Okay. Now we build the second one. About twelve feet in diameter. Right there." Scott stared at her, his mouth clenched. "A second one? Another ring? Are we summoning a smaller, angrier pig god to negotiate with the first one? My chiropractor is going to need a bigger boat."

Mike couldn't hold back a snicker this time. "Dad, just do what she says." "She's a witch, son." Scott whispered theatrically, grabbing a smaller branch. "We humor her, or she'll turn us into newts." The second, smaller ring of lighter branches was assembled much faster. Now they had two concentric rings of tied and twisted wood lying on the ground. Grace surveyed their work with a critical eye, walking the perimeter, her boots making soft crunching noises on the parched earth. "Good. It'll hold." She then unspooled more paracord. "Now for the fun part. Grab the three-foot poles. We're connecting the rings."

They watched as she flawlessly tied one of the shorter poles, positioning it so it slanted upwards from the outer ring to the inner, higher ring. The effect was immediate and clear. "Oh, I see," Scott said, a slow dawn of comprehension on his face. "It's a funnel. A big, wooden, upside-down… basket." "It's a corral," Grace corrected, already moving to the next position. "It creates a wide base but concentrates the trigger mechanism in the center. Now, tie them on. Every four feet. Make the knots tight."

For the next hour, the four of them worked, transforming the two flat circles into a massive, conical wooden skeleton. It rose from the ground like the framework of a rustic UFO, a testament to Grace's strange genius. Kyle tested one of the cross-beams with his full weight. "Solid construction. This will hold a lot more than pigs." As Grace tied filled sandbags to the cross members of the higher, smaller ring, Scott studied the trap intently. "How does the 'drop' part work, Grace?" Mike asked, genuinely curious as he cinched a knot.

Grace finished the coil, tucked the end neatly, and then let her gaze travel from the ground, up the three-foot support poles, to the pinnacle of their creation, and finally, higher still. With a slow, deliberate motion, she raised her hand and pointed a single, steady finger towards the canopy of the sprawling live oaks above them.

Scott followed her gesture, his eyes squinting against the nascent morning sun filtering through the leaves. He looked at the thick, interlocking branches, then back down at the conical cage, which had to weigh several hundred pounds with the added sandbags. A skeptical laugh escaped his lips. "With what? A skyhook? Did you pack an anti-gravity device in that little bag of yours, kid?" "We don't drop it," Grace said, her voice even and clear. "We release it." Scott's laugh was a dry, crackling sound in the humid Texas dawn. "Release it? Grace, honey, I appreciate the enthusiasm, but that thing weighs more most of us combined."

Grace didn't even smile. Her expression remained one of serene, unbothered focus. "We won't be lifting it with our backs, Scott. We'll be using physics." She gestured towards the thick, muscular branches of the live oaks arching over them. "The trees are our anchor points. We'll rig a three-point pulley system. The main load-bearing line will be secured with a toggle pin release. When the pigs come to feed, we trigger the trap, and the trap's own weight does the work."

Kyle, who had learned long ago not to question Grace's plans but simply to facilitate them, nodded slowly. "A deadfall trap, but inverted. Instead of dropping a weight onto something, we're dropping a cage around it. Brilliant." Mike's eyes were wide. "So it's like... a giant upside-down basket?" "Precisely," Grace said, a flicker of approval in her eyes. She then turned her attention to a large canvas bag and pulled out several spools of high-tensile rope. "While I rig the release mechanism and attach the netting, I need the three of you to gather bait."

Scott crossed his arms, his skepticism returning. "Alright, now you're talking my language. What do we got?

Old corn? A bag of soured mash? I know a thing or two about luring hogs." "No," Grace said. "Nothing that smells like us. We need local forage. Wild pigs in this area have a sweet tooth. Dewberries, mulberries, wild plums. They grow all along the creek beds. Fill your pouches. The more, the better. And crush some of them as you go to create a scent trail leading back here."

Scott opened his mouth, then closed it. He glanced at Kyle, who just gave him a slight shrug that clearly meant, 'Just do it, man.' Defeated by teenage ingenuity, Scott grunted. "Fine. Berries it is. C'mon, Mike. Let's go pick flowers for the pigs." For the next hour, the clearing was a hive of quiet, purposeful activity. Grace worked with a startling efficiency, her small hands deftly weaving rope through the wooden frame and securing the heavy netting. The conical trap began to look less like a skeleton and more like a massive, misplaced bug net, something you'd use to catch a pterodactyl.

Meanwhile, a few hundred yards away, the three men foraged. "I can't believe we're picking berries," Scott muttered, pushing a branch aside. "I've gutted hundreds of hogs. You know what's usually in their stomachs? Roots. Grubs. The occasional rattlesnake. Not... whatever these are." He held up a handful of dark purple berries.

"Those are dewberries," Kyle said, his pouch already half-full. "And Grace is right. They go crazy for them this time of year. It's like candy." "She's always right, isn't she?" Scott grumbled, though there was a note of grudging respect in his voice. "It's unnerving. She looks at a bunch of trees and sees a pulley system. I look at trees and see firewood and a place to hang a deer."

Mike, who had scrambled partway up a gnarled mulberry tree, called down, "Hey, Dad! These are way better over here! They're all ripe!" He was enjoying himself, the grim reality of their world momentarily forgotten in the simple pleasure of a scavenger hunt. Scott watched his son for a moment, a faint smile touching his lips. It beat the alternative. "Alright, hotshot. Don't eat 'em all. Those are for the bacon."

They returned to the clearing with pouches bulging with dark, sweet-smelling berries. Grace had finished her work. The trap was now a single, netted unit, with three ropes extending from its apex and threaded through heavy-duty carabiners she'd secured to the thickest oak limbs. The ends of the ropes were gathered together, ready to be hoisted. "Success, I see," Grace noted, her observant gaze flicking to Mike's stained mouth and then to the bulging pouches each man carried.

"We got your pig candy," Scott grumbled, unhitching his pouch and dropping it with a heavy thud. The sweet, wine-like scent of crushed berries filled the air. "I still say a pile of fermented corn mash would do the trick faster." "It would," Grace agreed calmly, "but it would also attract raccoons, opossums, and every deer in a five-mile radius. We want pigs, not a petting zoo. The specific terpene profile in ripe dewberries is a powerful selective attractant for suidae."

Scott just stared at her, blinking slowly. "The what-now in the whatsit?" Kyle clapped him on the shoulder. "She said pigs really, really like these berries, Scott." "I got that part," Scott muttered, glancing from the pile of ropes to the tiny fifteen-year-old commanding them. "Alright, Da Vinci. How are we supposed to get this whole mess up in the air? It's gonna take all four of us heaving on that rope."

Grace's expression was one of serene confidence, a stark contrast to Scott's gruff skepticism. She glanced from the thick coil of rope at her feet to the three much larger people standing before her, a small, almost imperceptible smile touching her lips. "It won't," she said, her voice soft but clear in the early morning air. "It'll take one of us."

Scott let out a short, incredulous bark of a laugh. "One of us? Kid, that net and the poles you wove into it have to weigh close to three hundred pounds. Even I couldn't just yank that up there, and I can press a whole hog." He gestured vaguely at his own broad chest and thick arms to emphasize the point. Mike, who had been quietly chewing on a berry, swallowed hard and looked between his father and the small-framed girl, his eyes wide.

"You're correct," Grace conceded, nodding. "The net assembly weighs approximately two hundred and seventy-five pounds. However, the problem isn't the mass of the trap." She picked up a shorter length of rope from her supplies. "The problem is my mass. I only weigh one hundred and ten pounds." Scott's face scrunched in confusion. "Okay... so what's your point? You're saying you're gonna lift it?" "Yes," Grace said simply. "But without proper anchoring, I'll lift myself off the ground before the trap gets more than a foot in the air."

Kyle chuckled, then stepped forward and put a reassuring hand on Scott's armored shoulder. "She's saying she's too light for how strong she is. She needs us to hold her down." Scott stared, his mouth slightly agape. He looked from Kyle's earnest face to Grace's placid one. "You're... you're serious?" he finally managed to stammer. Grace held the rope out to him. "Perfectly. Scott, I need you to take this rope, loop it securely through the carry handle on the back of my plate carrier, and then stand on the loose ends with both feet. Plant yourself. I need you to be an anchor."

Scott looked at the rope as if it were a snake. He glanced at Mike, who just shrugged, looking equally bewildered and fascinated. With a heavy, put-upon sigh that ruffled his beard, Scott took the rope. "Alright, Da Vinci," he muttered, kneeling behind Grace. The task felt utterly ridiculous. He was tying himself to a teenager to keep her from floating away. He threaded the rope through the carry handle of her body armor, pulled it snug, and dropped the ends to the ground. He placed one heavy boot firmly on the rope, then the other, spreading his stance like he was preparing to pull a truck out of the mud. "Okay. I'm... anchoring."

"Thank you," Grace said, turning her attention to Kyle. "Kyle, I need you to brace me from the front. A frontal bear hug, around my waist. Your job is to counteract any forward or upward pull that Scott's anchor point doesn't stabilize. Then hold on tight." Kyle chuckled, and stepped forward to stand in front of Grace. "Okay, Babe," Kyle said, his voice a mix of fond exasperation and genuine readiness. "Bracing from the front. What's the protocol?"

Instead of giving him instructions, Grace reached up, her hands finding the sides of his armor carrier. She pulled him down just enough to meet his lips with her own. It wasn't a long kiss, but it was firm and full of a quiet confidence that was so uniquely her. Scott made a sound that was half-choke, half-strangled gasp. "Are you kidding me? We're in the middle of... of... whatever this is, and you're... canoodling?"

Kyle pulled back, a grin spreading across his face. Grace didn't even blush. She simply looked back at Kyle, her expression now all business. "Okay. Ready?" She settled her feet. Kyle's smile softened into a look of focus. He wrapped his arms around her waist, his hands locking together over the small of her back. His stance was wide, his knees bent. It felt ridiculous, holding onto a fifteen-year-old girl like he was trying to stop her from shooting into orbit, but he'd learned long ago not to question Grace's physics. "Braced and ready," he confirmed. "Anchored," Scott grumbled from behind, the rope taut under his boots. "Mike, watch the pulleys," Grace instructed without looking at him. "Let me know if anything snags." "You got it, Grace," Mike said, his eyes wide with anticipation.

Grace took one deep, centering breath. Then, she leaned into her task. For Scott, the sensation was immediate and shocking. The rope went rigid, pulling with a force that made his feet slip. It wasn't a jerk; it was a smooth, inexorable pull, like he was the anchor point for a heavy-duty winch. He could feel the pressure through the thick soles of his boots, the earth compressing beneath him. He glanced down and saw the rope was vibrating with tension. This wasn't the strength of a girl. This wasn't even the strength of a man. This was something… else.

Kyle felt it too. A powerful forward and upward force pressed against his chest and arms. He just spread his legs wider. He felt Grace's core muscles engage, a solid wall of impossible power contained within her small frame. She wasn't straining, wasn't grunting. She was simply applying force in a way that defied logic.

Slowly, majestically, the massive pig net began to rise. A monstrous thing of wood, cordage, and camouflage netting that had taken them four hours to build, it lifted off the ground as if hoisted by an invisible crane. The pulleys they'd rigged to a thick oak branch creaked in protest, but held firm. Higher and higher it went, until it was suspended only three feet in the air, a shadowy canopy waiting to fall.

"Secure the rope!" Grace commanded, her voice perfectly even. Like a man shaking himself out of a trance, Mike quickly moved to tie off the main hoist rope to the base of the tree, his knots swift and sure. The tension released, and Scott stumbled forward a step, shaking his legs out. "Sweet mother of God," he breathed, staring from the suspended net to the slip of a girl who had just lifted it. He looked at his son. "You saw that, right? I'm not having a stroke?" Mike just nodded, his mouth still hanging open. "I saw it, Dad."

The silence that followed was thick enough to be a physical presence, broken only by the faint, stressed groan of the oak branch and the buzzing of early morning insects.

Scott stared at the suspended trap, a monstrous mesh of wood and rope hanging impossibly in the dappled sunlight. He ran a hand over his face, the rough Kevlar of his glove scraping against his cheeks.

"Okay," he said, his voice a low, gravelly rasp. "I've butchered hogs bigger than her. I've lifted engine blocks. I have never, in my forty-two years, seen anything like that." He turned his bewildered gaze from the trap to Grace, who was already brushing dirt from her hands as if she'd done nothing more strenuous than dusting a shelf. Kyle chuckled. "You get used to it." "Used to it?" Scott sputtered, gesturing wildly at Grace. "Kyle, she weighs like, a hundred pounds! She just... flexed on us!" Grace smiled. "It's really not that spectacular. Other than Poppy and Lucas, I'm the weakest of all my siblings."

Weakest. The word echoed in the cavern of Scott's skull, short-circuiting what was left of his rational brain. It was like a key turning in a lock, flinging open the door to a memory nearly two decades old. The sun wasn't a gentle dawn glow; it was a blistering, oppressive Texas glare. The air smelled of chlorine and sunscreen. He was twenty-two, between deployments, feeling invincible. He and his buddies, Parker, Eric, and a couple of others, were checking out the local talent at the waterpark, trying to forget the noise and dust of the desert. That's when he saw him. David. He was an island of calm in a sea of freakish children and surrounded by what seemed like a disproportionate number of beautiful women. Scott had watched, fascinated, as David effortlessly managed the sprawling group with a quiet word here, a gentle touch there.

Later, fueled by a cocktail of testosterone, and genuine curiosity, Scott and his friends had approached their picnic area. David, who looked to be in his late twenties then, had just smiled, a disarmingly warm expression. He wasn't threatened or offended, just... amused. "Gentlemen, welcome, please have a seat."

The invitation had stunned them into silence. Before they could answer, David had gestured to a couple of his sons, nearly toddlers at the time. " Brian, you and David drag that other picnic table over here, these men are going to join us for dinner." Scott remembered smirking, about to offer to help the kids with the impossible task. The table was one of those heavy-duty park models, solid wood planks and a steel frame. It had to weigh three hundred pounds, easy.

Then he watched as the two little boys trotted over to the empty table. They each grabbed an end, their tiny hands barely fitting around the planks. With a synchronized grunt that was almost comical, they lifted it. They lifted it and carried it across twenty feet of grass as if it were made of painted plastic, setting it down gently beside their own. The whole group of soldiers had stood there, slack-jawed, while David just continued grilling meat as if his 'toddlers' hadn't just violated several laws of physics.

"Dad? You okay?" Mike's voice snapped Scott back to the present. The sun was higher now, its warmth more insistent. The memory, so vivid and strange, receded, leaving behind a chilling, profound understanding. He looked at

Kyle, whose eyes held a knowing look. Of course Kyle was used to it. He'd probably seen her pull this shit before.

Scott's gaze drifted back to Grace. She had finished with the bait. After digging a couple of small holes with a trowel and burying some of the sweet, fermented berries to draw the pigs in with a lingering scent, she'd had Mike dump the rest in a pile right under the drop-cage. Now, she was doing something even more unbelievable.

Effortlessly, she shimmied up the thick trunk of the oak tree, moving with the speed and confidence of a squirrel. She didn't use footholds; she just seemed to glide upwards. Reaching the thick branch where the pulley was anchored, she took the trip rope and, with a few deft movements, tied a complex knot just before the pulley, a quick-release hitch. She tugged it once to ensure it was secure, then patted the rope. One solid yank on the other end, hidden in the brush fifty yards away, and the knot would unbind, allowing the rope to slide freely and the cage to fall.

She slid back down the tree and landed silently on her feet. Then picked up her AR-10, settled it comfortably in her hands, and looked at the three of them. "All set," she announced sweetly. "Now we just have to untie the suspension rope, be quiet and wait." Scott looked from the impossibly strong fifteen-year-old girl to her massive rifle, then to the perfectly constructed trap. He looked at his son, who was staring at Grace with pure, unadulterated hero worship. Finally, he looked at Kyle, who was picking dry leaves off his pants.

Scott let out a long, slow breath. "Right," he said, his voice strangely calm. "Weakest." He shook his head, a wry, defeated smile touching his lips. He was living in a world run by the children of whatever David was, and he was on a team with the 'weakest' one. Suddenly, trapping a few wild hogs seemed like the most normal thing he'd do all day.

Chapter 24:

The Sniper's Bullet

Grace dusted the bark and leaf litter from her hands, the motion as simple and unconcerned as if she'd just finished potting a plant. She looked at the three men, her expression bright and sweet. "Well, I'm starving," she announced cheerfully. "Is it lunchtime yet?"

Scott just stared for a moment. "Lunch?" he finally managed, the word sounding foreign. "We... we just..." He gestured vaguely at the massive deadfall cage hanging precariously from the branch. "Yeah! I could eat!" Mike piped up, his eyes still wide with awe as he stared at Grace. To him, she hadn't just set a trap; she'd rearranged the universe to her liking, and now she was graciously suggesting a snack break. It was one of the coolest things he had ever seen.

Kyle grinned and unslung Grace's pack. He was long past the point of being surprised by anything a child of David's could do. "Way ahead of you," he said, rummaging inside. He produced a large, sealed plastic bag filled with what looked suspiciously like oatmeal cookies. "David sent us off with a batch of his oatmeal-raisin demolition charges." He shook the bag, the cookies clacking together softly. "And I've got trail mix and beef jerky. Standard apocalyptic picnic fare."

He gestured with his head towards a small, shady grove of live oaks about twenty-five yards away from their current position. "We can post up over there. It's got good cover." Grace's eyes followed his gesture, her gaze analytical. The sweet, hungry teenager was once again replaced by the observant strategist. "Those trees will work," she agreed, nodding. "We can get a good vantage point up there, and our scent will be higher off the ground. The pigs won't know we're here until it's too late. Plus, it's close enough to release the trap." She gave Kyle a brilliant smile. "Good idea."

Scott just stared. Of course. They weren't just going for a picnic. They were establishing an elevated, scent-masked, tactical lunch position. "Right then," Kyle said, slinging his pack back over his shoulder. "Let's move." The four of them picked their way quietly through the scrub. They reached the grove, a cool, shaded oasis, where Grace immediately picked the largest, most centrally located oak.

"This one's perfect," she declared, before once again launching herself up the trunk. She moved with the same impossible, frictionless grace, her small frame finding purchase where there was none. In seconds, she was settled on a thick limb seven feet up, her legs dangling as she accepted the pack Kyle passed up to her.

Mike, determined not to be outdone and fueled by a fourteen-year-old's potent combination of adrenaline and ambition, started scrambling up after her. His ascent was considerably less elegant, involving a lot more grunting, scraped knees, and boots scrabbling noisily for holds. "Easy there, hotshot," Kyle chuckled, watching him. "Don't spook the bacon."

Scott leaned his AR-15 against the base of the tree and sank down, running a hand through his sweat-damp hair. He watched his son finally heave himself onto a lower branch, breathing hard but beaming with pride. Grace was already handing him a cookie. Kyle stayed on the ground with Scott, leaning against the neighboring tree and pulling out a cookie for himself. He offered the bag to Scott. "You're awfully quiet," Kyle noted, taking a large bite. "Everything okay?"

Scott took a cookie, then stared at the pastry in his hand. It looked so normal. So mundane. "Kyle," he began, his voice low. "She... she climbs like a squirrel. She sets traps like a master engineer. She's fifteen and carrying a rifle that could stop a truck. And she calls it being the 'weakest'." He finally looked at Kyle, his eyes pleading for some kind of rational explanation in an irrational world. "You're marrying her. Does any of this feel... I don't know... weird to you?"

Kyle chewed his cookie thoughtfully for a moment, then swallowed. "Weird?" he repeated. He looked up at Grace, who was now patiently explaining the best way to distribute his weight on a branch to a rapt Mike. A genuinely fond smile touched Kyle's lips. "Nah. It was weird for maybe the first few months I was on the ranch. Now, it's just... life." He took another bite. "Look, David's not exactly a normal guy, so his kids aren't gonna be normal. Even you should be used to it by now." He nudged Scott with his elbow. "Besides, would you rather be out here with a bunch of regular, scared teenagers, or with her?"

Scott nodded slowly, the weight of Kyle's logic settling in his shoulders like a heavy pack. Kyle was right. Given the choice between a typical, terrified group of teenagers and... well, Grace, the answer was obvious. He'd take the miniature spec-ops soldier every time. It was just the mental whiplash of it all that got to him. Grace simply didn't look the part.

He finally brought the cookie to his lips and took a bite, his mind still chewing on the absurdity. For a fraction of a second, there was the familiar, comforting taste of a good, homemade oatmeal cookie. Then, it was like a culinary flashbang went off on his tongue. The first bite was a lie. A beautiful, buttery, oaty lie. For a glorious half-second, Scott's brain registered Oatmeal Cookie. It was a comforting, nostalgic signal from a world that no longer existed, a taste of church bake sales and afternoon snacks. Then the flashbang detonated.

His chewing slowed, then stopped entirely, his jaw frozen mid-motion. His eyes, which had been fixed on the half-moon of cookie in his hand, widened in alarm. It wasn't a single flavor that assaulted him, but a coordinated, multi-pronged attack on his taste buds. First came the flanking maneuver of toasted almonds and the earthy crunch of walnuts. Before he could process that, a tropical insurgency of shredded coconut launched a surprise raid. Then, the heavy artillery landed, a sticky, sweet barrage of raisins and tart cranberries, all of it bound together not by simple sugar, but by a dense, floral tide of honey that coated his entire mouth.

It wasn't bad. That was the most terrifying part. It was… delicious. But it was a chaotic, lawless deliciousness. It was a cookie that had looked at the very definition of "cookie" and decided to wage a one-pastry war against it. It had the texture of a dense energy bar but the soul of a grandmother's secret recipe. It was a delicious abomination.

Scott turned his gaze from the culinary paradox in his hand and looked to Kyle, his expression a desperate plea for an explanation. Kyle, however, was merely watching him with a knowing, infuriatingly calm smirk. "What's wrong now, Dad?" Mike asked, leaning over. He had already devoured his own cookie without a moment's hesitation and had a few crumbs clinging to his chin. "You look like you just saw a centipede."

"Worse, Mike," Scott managed to croak, finally forcing his jaw to work again. He swallowed the mouthful of complex carbohydrates. "I think I just ate one." He held up the offending baked good. "What... in the name of all that is holy and leavened... is this?" A light thud sounded behind them. Grace had dropped from the oak branch as silently as a falling leaf. She landed in a perfect crouch before springing up, brushing dust from her pants. She was wearing a faint, proud smile. "Oh! You mean Daddy's Energy Cookies?" she said, her voice bright and clear. "Do you like them? I made this batch myself."

"You... you made this?" Scott asked, his voice softer now, laced with a new layer of bewilderment. "Yep!" Grace beamed. "I followed Daddy's recipe exactly. It's got oatmeal, and the special flour mix, you know, the one with wheat, millet, lentils, beans, barley, and rye. Then there's fresh honey, shredded coconut, coconut oil, raisins, cranberries, and a whole bunch of almonds and walnuts for extra protein. It's designed for maximum caloric density and sustained energy release over a four-to-six-hour period." She recited the information with the rote precision of a student who had aced her finals.

Scott stared at her, then back at Kyle. Kyle's smirk had blossomed into a full-blown grin. "What she said," Kyle confirmed, taking a leisurely bite of his own cookie. "David figured out that a single cookie could replace a full MRE in terms of energy, but with better macronutrient balance and without the chemical aftertaste."

"Chemical aftertaste?" Scott sputtered, gesturing wildly with the cookie. "Kyle, this thing tastes like a granola bar had a baby with a bag of trail mix and they raised it in a bird-feeder! It has beans, Kyle. Beans! In a cookie! That's not food, that's an agricultural experiment gone rogue." Mike, sensing his father's befuddlement, piped up, "Can I have yours, then?" "No!" Scott snapped, pulling the cookie protectively to his chest plate. His survival instincts warred with his culinary principles. It was an abomination, yes, but Grace had also mentioned 'sustained energy release,' and they could be out here for hours waiting for the feral hogs to take the bait in their corral trap. He wasn't about to get woozy because of his stubborn palate.

"He gets like this," Kyle explained to Grace, who was now looking slightly concerned. "He grew up in a world of simple food. Flour, sugar, butter. The concept of a cookie being a survival tool is… jarring for him." "It's not jarring, it's just wrong!" Scott insisted, taking another, smaller, more suspicious bite. Damn it all, it was still delicious. He hated it. He hated that he liked it. "A cookie is supposed to be a treat. Simple. Comforting. This… this is a brick. A nutritionally complete, surprisingly palatable, raisin-studded brick. It's an insult to the entire concept of dessert."

Grace blinked, processing his tirade with the serene calm that often unnerved people. "But it's not dessert, Scott," she said, her voice soft but clear. "It's mission fuel. The lentils and the six-grain flour blend create a complete protein. The fats from the coconuts and nuts and the complex carbs from the oatmeal are formulated for slow-burn energy so we don't crash. And the specific ratios make it a nootropic stack."

Scott froze mid-chew, his eyes widening. "A noo-what?" he mumbled through a mouthful of walnuts and treasonous beans. He swallowed hard. "A nootropic stack? What in the Sam Hill is a nootropic? Is that one of them fancy mushrooms? Did David weaponize fungus and put it in our snacks?" Mike stifled a laugh. "It means it's brain food, Dad. Helps you focus."

"I'm plenty focused!" Scott retorted, a little too loudly. He pointed his cookie accusingly at Kyle. "You see what's happening? She's violated the sanctity of the cookie. It's supposed to be dumb food. Happy food. Now it's… thinking food." Kyle chuckled, leaning his AR-15 against the tree trunk beside him. "I don't know, Scott. My brain feels pretty normal. Maybe you should have another one, help you think of better insults."

"Blasphemy!" Scott declared, finishing the last bite of his cookie and carefully wiping the crumbs from his tactical vest. "That's what this is. To call these… these cognitive enhancement wafers a 'cookie' is a culinary sacrilege. It's an affront to God and Betty Crocker. It's a lie wrapped in an

215

enigma, baked at 350 degrees of pure deception." He paused, his rant seemingly coming to a dramatic conclusion. He took a deep breath, his eyes locking onto the canvas bag sitting next to Kyle. "Give me another one." Mike snorted. "I thought it was blasphemy, Dad."

Scott pointed a finger at his son, his other hand already reaching for the bag Kyle held out. "It is! But one must study thine enemy to defeat it. I'm engaging in... culinary reconnaissance." He plucked another one of David's controversial oatmeal cookies from the bag and examined it. "Look at it. So unassuming. Posing as a simple treat, yet inside it's a Trojan horse of lentils and intellectual superiority."

After the intellectual crisis of the super-cookies was muted, a comfortable silence settled over the oak grove. The sweltering Texas sun beat down, the heat shimmering in waves above the dry grass. The only sounds were the lazy drone of insects and the occasional rustle of leaves in the light breeze. Kyle kept a casual watch, Scott continued to lean against a thick trunk looking for all the world like he was about to nap, and Mike fidgeted, trying to emulate the practiced stillness of the adults.

Hours passed. The shadows of the oaks stretched long and distorted across the ground. Just as Mike was about to whisper a complaint about the boredom, he saw Grace shift. It was barely a movement, just a slow tilt of her head, her eyes fixed on the brush to their left. She raised a single, steady hand, palm flat. Stop. Listen. Instantly, Scott was awake and alert, his hand resting on his rifle. Kyle brought his own weapon to a low ready, his gaze following Grace's. A moment later, they heard it, the faint but unmistakable sound of twigs snapping and low, guttural snuffling.

Grace didn't move. Her breathing was even, her focus absolute. The rustling grew louder, and then, from the thicket, a massive, bristly boar emerged. It sniffed the air, its dark little eyes scanning the clearing before it trotted confidently towards the baited corral. It was followed by two large sows and then, a chaotic, tumbling stream of tiny, striped piglets. They squealed and shoved at each other, a whirlwind of miniature energy, swarming the pile of sweet berries inside the trap. "Holy Moses," Mike breathed, his eyes wide.

Grace held up a hand again, her index finger extended. Wait. She waited, her patience like stone, as the last wriggling piglet scrambled under the raised gate. When the entire sounder was milling about, completely engrossed in the feast, her hand moved with fluid precision. She gave a sharp, decisive tug on the cord wrapped around her wrist.

The cord went taut in Grace's hand, and with a heavy THUMP, the gate of the corral dropped, sealing the entire sounder inside. The pigs panicked for a moment, a chorus of startled grunts and squeals echoing through the oak grove, but the lure of the sweet berries was too strong. Within seconds, they were back to feasting.

Grace didn't wait. She rushed forward, and with the fluid economy of motion that defined her, she raised a tranquilizer gun. Three soft thwips punctuated the air, almost too quiet to hear over the contented snuffling of the pigs. The massive boar was the first to stagger, its head drooping into the berry pile before it keeled over with a soft oof. The two sows followed moments later, collapsing into a twitching, bristly heap. The fifteen piglets barely noticed, climbing over their slumbering mothers to get better access to the food.

The other three rose from their hiding spot, the tension of the hunt replaced by a stunned silence as they approached the trap. "Holy crap, Grace," Mike breathed, his eyes wide as he stared at the scene. He pointed a trembling finger. "That was... holy crap." He started counting the piglets, his voice a disbelieving whisper. "One... two... three... holy Moses, there's fifteen of them! Fifteen!"

Scott watched, his jaw slightly unhinged, as his son had what appeared to be a complete system failure over the number of piglets in the pen. He himself, a man who'd spent considerable time around livestock, had never seen a trap go off so perfectly, so... bloodlessly. He clapped a heavy hand on Mike's shoulder, a gesture meant to be grounding. "Breathe, son. You're gonna hyperventilate."

Grace paid them no mind, her focus already on the next phase. "Kyle," she said, her voice calm and clear over the oinking of the piglets. "The Beast. Bring it up, trunk facing the corral. "Yes, ma'am," Kyle answered with an easy grin, already turning to jog back toward the tree line where they'd hidden the car. With a careful slide of the net, Grace slipped inside the corral, moving with a quiet confidence that soothed the agitated piglets. She produced a yellow oil-based paint marker from one of her cargo pockets.

One by one, she gently cornered a piglet, running a practiced hand over its back and legs, checking its confirmation. She peered into its eyes, ensuring they were clear and bright. "What are you looking for, exactly?" Scott asked, leaning against the corral frame. "Healthy stock," Grace replied without looking up. She drew a neat yellow line down the back of a particularly stout-looking male. "Good length, straight legs, no signs of runting. We want breeders, not just porkers. This one has good shoulders." She nudged her first choice toward a corner and moved on to the next.

Mike watched, mesmerized. "It's like she's picking out puppies." Kyle handled the Beast with surprising finesse, easing it over the uneven terrain until it was parked just a few feet from the corral, its trunk yawning open. Kyle hopped out, dusting off his hands. "One off-road capable pig-mobile, as requested." Grace gave a single, sharp nod of approval. She reached into another of her seemingly endless cargo pockets and produced a small, vacuum-sealed bag filled with what looked like miniature, brown, pellet-like cubes.

Scott squinted, his practical butcher's mind trying to process the scene. "What in the world is that? You're gonna give them candy?" "Medicated bait," Grace corrected. She deftly unsealed the bag, releasing a faint, sweet scent of molasses. "A mild sedative mixed with corn mash. It'll make them drowsy and docile. Easier to transport, less stress on the animal." Mike's eyes widened. "So… pig roofies?" Scott shot his son a look. "Mike. Don't call it that."

Ignoring the exchange, Grace slipped back into the corral with the seven marked piglets. The piglets, trusting and hungry, snuffled the treats from her palm and chomped down. their chewing slowing within seconds. The effect was immediate and, frankly, hilarious. The small section of the corral soon looked like a piglet nursery after a very long, very satisfying naptime. "Alright," Grace announced, stepping out and securing the gate. "Let's get them loaded."

After releasing the sandbags, Grace lifted the corner of the corral. It's lightened mass, now a third of the original weight. She pushed it aside, creating a wide opening. The few piglets that hadn't been marked or sedated squealed in alarm and scrambled back to the reassuring, albeit unconscious, bulk of their mothers. "Okay, two at a time," Grace instructed. She slipped back to the sounder and gently scooped up a snoozing, spotted piglet. It was limp as a sack of flour, letting out a soft, wheezing snore.

Scott moved with a surprising gentleness. He picked up another sedated piglet, holding it away from his body armor as if it were a fragile, ticking bomb. "Never thought I'd be a pig-napper," he murmured, carrying it over to the open trunk of the Beast. One by one, they transferred the seven drowsy piglets into the specially prepared cages in the trunk.

Mike watched, leaning against the fender of the car. "It's like a clown car, but for pigs," he observed. "A pork-us." Scott shot him a look that was half-amusement, half-exasperation. "Just… help Kyle keep an eye on the perimeter, son." As Scott placed the last piglet in its cage, Grace didn't move to close the trunk. Instead, she stood with her hands on her hips, surveying the pile of sleeping hogs. Her young face was set in a thoughtful, almost clinical expression. "We're not done," she announced.

Scott wiped a bead of sweat from his brow. "Not done? Grace, we've got seven of 'em snoozing in the trunk.

The job's done. Let's get back before this heat cooks us in our own armor." "It looks done," Grace corrected, her voice calm and even. She gestured towards the remaining unconscious hogs. "But think about it. If another group, one as smart as us, found this scene, what would they see? A whole sounder, minus seven piglets. That's not natural predation. A coyote or a bobcat might get one, maybe two. This," she swept her hand over the sleeping pigs, "this is a kidnapping. It's a sign that an organized, intelligent group was here. It leaves a trail."

Kyle, who had been silently observing from the side, nodded slowly. He saw the logic. It was the kind of long-term, strategic thinking David had drilled into all of them. "So what's the play?" he asked, his eyes following Grace's. "We take a sow," Grace stated. "A big one. If a sow leaves with half her litter, it just looks like the sounder split. It's a natural occurrence. It masks our actions."

Scott stared at her, then at the car, then back at Grace. "Take a sow? Grace, these aren't piglets. That one," he pointed a finger at the largest sow, a beast easily weighing over two hundred pounds, "is bigger than Mike. Then he remembered who he was talking to. "Fine," he sighed, the word thick with resignation. He gave a mock bow, a dip of his head full of sarcasm and a strange, undeniable respect. "Go ahead, your highness."

Grace gave him a small, appreciative smile, completely unbothered by his tone. "Thank you, Scott. It's the smart play." She turned to the car. "Blanket first. We don't want to scratch Aidan's paint." She retrieved a thick moving blanket from the back seat, shaking it out with a snap. Kyle, already

221

anticipating the next step, grabbed a pair of heavy-duty ratchet straps.

Grace approached the sow, which weighed a solid two hundred and fifty pounds, and crouched as Scott and Mike watched. There was no grunt of effort, no visible strain. She simply hooked her hands under the sow's considerable girth and stood up, lifting the animal as if it were a large sack of dog food. She walked calmly to the back of the Beast and, with a soft thump, placed the unconscious sow directly onto the trunk lid.

The methodical click-click-click of the ratchet strap was the only sound breaking the afternoon's insectile hymn. Kyle cinched the last strap tight, the heavy nylon digging into the unconscious sow's bristly hide. He gave it a solid shove. The pig didn't budge, but the Beast's suspension groaned in protest. "Aidan's gonna kill me," he muttered, wiping a bead of sweat from his brow with the back of his hand. "Strapping a two-hundred-and-fifty-pound hog to his baby."

As he worked, Grace's attention, once filled with a mixture of amusement and tactical satisfaction, had drifted. The easy smile faded from her lips. She stood perfectly still, her head cocked slightly, her eyes fixed on the dense, shadowy line of cypress and oak trees about a hundred yards away. The AR-10, which had been resting casually in the crook of her arm, came up in one fluid, economical motion, the stock settling against her shoulder as if it were a natural extension of her body. Her entire demeanor had shifted from a sweet fifteen-year-old to a seasoned predator.

"Kyle," she said, her voice low and tight, cutting through the heat. "Someone's out there. Watching us." The air went cold. Scott, who had been leaning against the rear fender, straightened up instantly, his hand going to the grip of his own AR-15. His face, moments before crinkled in weary amusement, was now a mask of hard-bitten focus. His gaze snapped to his son. "Mike, get in the car. Now!" he barked, the command absolute. Mike didn't hesitate, scrambling over the seat and ducking down in the back, his own rifle clutched in a white-knuckled grip. "Grace, Kyle, move! Get in!"

The world dissolved into a blur of frantic motion. Kyle spun away from the trunk, turning towards the driver's side door just as Grace pivoted to do the opposite. For a split second, they were a clumsy tangle of limbs and body armor, crossing paths in the scant few feet of open space beside the car. CRACK.

The sound wasn't a boom, but a sharp, vicious tear in the fabric of the day. It was followed instantly by a violent, sledgehammer-like blow to Kyle's right shoulder. The impact spun him, a grunt of raw pain and shock tearing from his throat. Fiery agony exploded from his collarbone, a searing heat that was completely alien to the day's warmth. His arm went numb, the Glock on his hip feeling a thousand pounds heavier. He stumbled, his knee hitting the dusty ground, his mind struggling to process the searing pain that radiated down his arm and across his chest. He'd been hit, just outside the protection of his plate carrier.

Kyle looked at his hand, the blood already spilling down his arm. But he hadn't been the only one. Grace was directly in front of him, her shoulder to him as she moved for the door. The bullet, having ripped through the flesh and muscle of Kyle's shoulder, had continued its trajectory. It struck her in the back of her left shoulder, punching through her arm and into her body.

Her body did not crumple; it unraveled. With a sudden, shocking finality, all life and tension drained from her limbs. Her collapse was absolute, a marionette whose strings had been severed all at once. Her eyes rolled back as she fell, landing in a still, silent heap on the ground. The heavy AR-10, an extension of her will only a second before, clattered uselessly beside her, a sudden piece of scrap metal in the dirt.

For an eternal heartbeat, the world held its breath. The only sounds were the low, guttural rumble of the Beast's engine and the frantic, shallow panting of Mike from within the vehicle. Kneeling nearby, Kyle's own ragged gasps were swallowed by a rising tide of horror as he stared at Grace's utterly still form. The world fractured into a series of movements like burning static as he and Scott scrambled, fueled by adrenaline and dread, to get her into the car. The burnout that followed kicked up a plume of dust so thick it seemed to swallow the remaining sunlight, leaving them in a world of their own making.

Inside the speeding vehicle, the world became a screaming, crimson blur. Kyle's left hand was a white-knuckled claw on the steering wheel, his right arm a useless, burning appendage. A deafening drumbeat of pain throbbed in his shoulder, but it was nothing, a distant echo, compared to the roaring silence from the passenger seat beside him. He risked a glance, a single, sideways turn of his head that felt as though it might shatter his soul.

Grace was slumped against the door, held upright only by the thin strap of her seatbelt. Her face, usually so alive with fierce intelligence and humor, was ashen, a deathly mask of bleached bone. And the blood. God, the blood. A dark, wet stain on her body armor was spreading with sickening speed, a crimson flower blooming over her shoulder and chest. Her head lolled to the side, her hair a shroud obscuring her features, but the utter lack of tension in her form was a scream in itself. She was a doll, dropped and forgotten.

Is she breathing? The thought was not a question but a shard of ice plunging into his heart. God, is she even breathing? The silence from her corner of the world was his answer, an abyss of terror that threatened to consume him whole. This was his fault. This was his reckoning. The bullet had come for him, and in the space of a single second, Grace had paid the price.

"What happened?! DAD! WHAT HAPPENED TO GRACE?!" Mike's adolescent voice cracked, a shriek of raw terror from the back seat that cut through Kyle's pain-fogged haze. "Mike, stay back! Stay buckled!" Scott's voice was a low growl. He unbuckled, bracing himself against the violent sway of the Beast as Kyle pushed it to its limits. Scott leaned over the seat, his eyes taking in the same horrifying tableau that had seared itself onto Kyle's soul: Grace, limp and pale, the crimson stain on her armor spreading like a nightmare.

"Kyle, what the hell was that?!" Scott yelled, his hands hovering uselessly over Grace, afraid to touch, afraid not to. "Sniper!" Kyle bit out, his jaw clenched so tight he felt his teeth might crack. He didn't dare take his eyes off the blur of the road. "Bullet went through me and into her! We gotta get back!" Scott's hand finally found the side of Grace's neck, pressing into the soft skin below her jawline. His face, already grim, turned to stone. His voice dropped, suddenly hollow and cold. "Kyle... I don't feel a pulse." A choked sob erupted from Mike in the back.

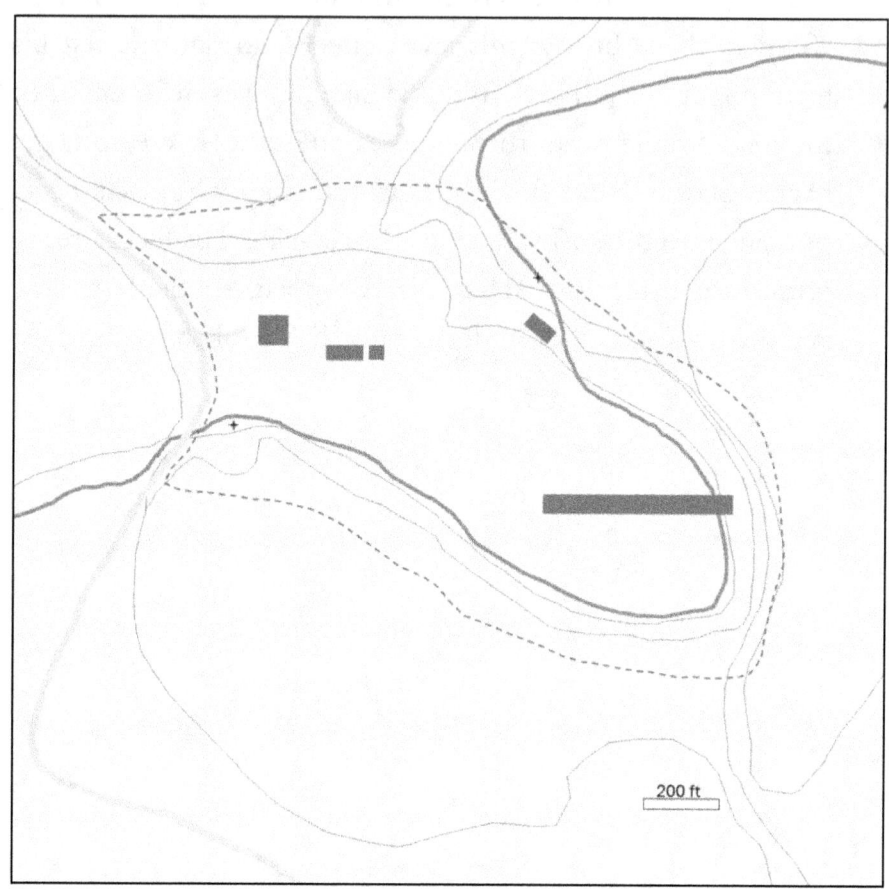

David's Valley

Oatmeal Raisin Demolition Charges

Flour and Grain –

2 ½ cups wheat grain or hard white grain

1 ½ cups spelt or fitch

½ cup hulled barley.

¼ cup millet

¼ cup lintels

2 tbsp each kidney, pinto northern beans

Other ingredients –

6 ½ cup whole oats

4 cups of honey

5 large eggs

2 cups of virgin coconut oil

½ cup of water

1 ½ tbsp baking powder

1 tsp salt

Filler ingredients –

1 cup crushed walnuts

1 cup cut almonds

1 cup raisins

1 cup craisins (dried cranberries)

1 cup desiccated coconut